The Guide to Being a Dictator's Mistress

Cedrick Mendoza-Tolentino

ISBN: 978-1-956692-22-8

Acknowledgements

Alphabetica: The Other Side of Love was the winner of the First Annual Chuck Kinder Honorary Chapbook Prize and was published by Corgi Snorkel Press.

The Dictator was published in *Joyland*.

The Food Truck Owner was published in the Mondays are Murder series by Akashic Books.

The Guide to Being a Dictator's Body Double was published and performed by *Liars' League*.

The Guide to Being a Dictator's Mistress and In Character were published and performed by *Liars' League New York*.

The Jesus Fish and That Wedding Dress were published in *Gargoyle Magazine*.

Mikhail was published in *Plain Spoke*.

Seeing is Believing was published in *The Nottingham Review*.

Teddy was published in *Reflection's Edge*.

Table of Contents

The Guide to Being a Dictator's Mistress

1. Never fall in love with him.

2. Do not give in to his initial advances, no matter how insistent he is. Ignore the tramps, whores, and prostitutes who think that the path to riches lies somewhere beneath his sheets. He will be generous with them—initially—bathing and covering them with scented oils and floral soaps. They will think that they are being pampered—loved even—while he will wonder why he cannot make them smell like his wife did when they first met. When he realizes that he has done everything he can with them, explored everything there is to discover, he will dispose of them like used Kleenex. The moment he casts them aside, his guards and "trusted" advisers will swoop in for their turn. No, you must not give in immediately. Instead, reveal yourself slowly, as if you hold all the power in this most paternalistic of courtship rituals. The longer it takes, the more he will look at you differently than the rest of the women he respects and even less than the woman who shares his name.

3. But do not take too long to grant him access to that space between your legs, or any other space to which he wants access. If he feels as if you are stringing him along or that

there is another man vying for your affection, you are just as likely to be beheaded and have your head mounted on a pike outside the palace as being pushed aside and ignored. Let Aristotle's Golden Mean be your guide. If you manage to play your cards right, you will have guaranteed years of comfortable living. Yes, there may be evenings where you are forced to do unspeakable things, the kinds of things that most people can only watch on a computer screen or television set. But ultimately, those evenings are worth it if, for the remainder of your time with him, you are treated as his "special one."

4. Once you are "in," or rather, he is "in," you must never travel in public unless you are dressed for an evening out with him. Those in his inner circles will whisper and bemoan how unbecoming it is for the father of our great Republic to be seen bedding some plain-faced commoner. You will not have the benefit of Photoshop, and people in the media who wish to make their displeasure with him known without eliciting retribution will attack you whenever they have the opportunity. Take the first few sums of money he showers on you to invest in some make-up and simple dresses. You will thank me later.

5. Tread lightly around those who have reason to hate you. His wife, of course, will tolerate you the way she tolerates the rats and insects she knows sometimes creep up from the cellar into the palace kitchens. Like those vermin that manage to find their way back to the dark shadows below the palace floor, be visible as little as possible. That is the only way to avoid being squashed by her. His family will look at you as a sign of his vices, which will not be the

worst of things, because it is the other vices people fear, the ones that result in people disappearing or counting their blessings when they lose only an arm or a thumb. Her family, though, will be different. They will hate you and every other woman who shares his bed that is not their little girl who loved her pigtails and her doll Krystal. Be wary of them. They may not have the power to do away with you—only he has the power to do that—but they can certainly make your life difficult. Best that you eliminate contact with them altogether. The rats and insects certainly do. Or at least the ones that live.

6. Unless absolutely necessary, never be away from him for more than a week at a time. He will inevitably spend a night or two with his wife, though that is fine because her frigid reception of him will only make him lust after you more. Allow him the occasional dalliance with someone else. It will further distinguish you from every other woman in his life and he will come to see you as a true companion, one that truly understands him. But be careful. If he finds someone who intrigues him more than you, you may find yourself barred from the palace after taking a short walk to get some air. The guards will look at you as they do the other discarded Kleenex girls, available to do with as they wish. No matter how much you protest and threaten ("He will cut off your balls for this!"), nothing will stop them. This is why it is of paramount importance to continue to live Aristotle's Golden Mean, keeping enough of a distance so that he continues to think of you as mysterious and desirable, a

woman who will continue to amaze him, but never so much that he forgets you altogether.

7. Accept every bauble, every trinket that he gives you. Never wonder where these came from or how they were paid for. If you were to learn they were his wife's, what would you do? If you were to learn that they were stolen from a shopkeeper, would you return them? And if you were to learn that their former owners were now buried 6 feet under, what would you do then? No, better that you accept everything he presents you with a smile and a kiss. If ever you are uncomfortable with those items, have someone sell them for you three or four cities away. You never want to be in the position of having to explain to him why one of his soldiers was able to purchase one of his gifts to you for his own mistress.

8. Reinvent your life history. Arrange for someone you trust to continue to send money to your family and loved ones, someone who is discreet and understands that while your family and loved ones need to know that you are fine, they do not need to know how you got that money. If your family did not need it, you would look at him as everyone else does—a lunatic drunk with power—rather than as a source of income. Few in the country live above the poverty line, unless they have found some way to work with him or exploit him. You have merely found your own way to do so.

9. Nod your head and smile whenever he says he loves you. Stroke his chin and giggle like a schoolgirl when he says that he has fallen deeply and madly in love with you. Tell him that he makes you happier than you have ever been

when he tells you that he is going to leave his wife for you ("She is too close-minded. If only I had met you earlier. It should be you at my side."). Enjoy the feelings that come with so powerful a man falling in love with you. But never forget that these are merely words, one of the many weapons he wields as easily as the sword and pistol he wears on his belt. He will never leave her for you no matter what he promises. A man like him does not come into power by keeping his promises.

10. Under no circumstances can you get pregnant. Too many terrible things can happen if you carry his child within you. His enemies will look at you as a way to hurt him, while his family will try their best to make tragedy strike. If your family ever heard, they would disown you. And this does not even account for the most dangerous reaction of all—his. There is no telling how he will respond with the knowledge that you will be another incubator for his seed. He will have sent away all the others careless enough to get pregnant, who are forced to battle morning sickness and the thickening of their bodies. You will be no different—once your belly swells, he will no longer have any use for you. The only way that you can ensure your safety and your livelihood is to ensure that nothing ever gains a foothold in your womb. Do whatever it takes to ensure that never happens.

11. When you hear that he has been killed, that his body has been torn asunder, remain cool and indifferent to the news. When the whole country rejoices and the world's papers speak of a new era of hope and change, do not celebrate with them, but do not mourn his passing either.

If you do, the mobs will come for you too. If you rejoice the way everyone else will, they will look at you as a hypocrite, someone who will do anything or say anything to be spared. You do not want to find yourself dangling from a rope. Take a cue from his enemies that managed to survive—stay quiet, and whenever someone keeps pressing you, say that you are not comfortable discussing the subject. It will mean that when it is finally safe to say something, in those final years when people will make any excuse to be patient with that terrible man's favorite mistress, you will never have to fear the angry shouts, insults, and spit that those who stepped forward in his defense had to bear.

12. And if you forget any of the preceding, you have nothing to worry about, so long as you remember the most important rule of all: Never fall in love with him.

The Guide to Being a Dictator's Body Double

1. Accept your fate. Accept that the series of unlikely events and occurrences that culminated in you did in fact happen and would in fact make a wonderful story, the kind that, over time, was thought of and shared as myth or legend. Accept that your story is the kind of story that people often heard and wondered what parts, however small, were actually true—the way that your parents' DNA fit together in that particular configuration just so; the year and country of your birth; and of course, the unfortunate fact that you were playing in front of your parents' home at the exact moment that a caravan of soldiers returning to the capital happened to pass by, and that one of the soldiers, having decided not to partake in the usual victory libations, took one look at you and instantly recognized the uncanny resemblance between you and the son of their country's inspirational leader and father to all. All of this had to happen exactly so. Please, accept your fate— the sooner you do, the sooner you will be able to find peace, even if that peace comes while you pretend to be, and everyone believes you to be, someone else.

2. Study him at every opportunity—or her, if gender equality has finally reached this most ancient of professions. You must not only understand the things that he does in public when all eyes and all cameras are on him, but you must understand all the things that he does when no one is looking. Your ability to *be* him, to exude him, even when no one is looking, will be what makes you successful in your role. Like all great character actors—the ones who become synonymous with the roles that they play—you must become the "him" that everyone imagines when they hear his name.

3. You must not only study him, but you must also study all the things that he studies. It will be important that you know all the same historical facts that he does, all of the same chronologies that should make him realize that if history follows its standard course for autocrats, it will take more than a body double to save his own life.

4. Do not let people see the two of you together too often. That would defeat your purpose. However similar you are to him physically, you are not his identical twin—you may be able to fool the people who only see him on television or from a distance at a rally, carelessly shooting bullets into the air, oblivious to the very real possibility that some of those gathered may be hit by those bullets on their way back down, but those will be the only ones. Anyone who has had more than a superficial glimpse will recognize you as an imposter immediately. And unfortunately for you, many of the people who could differentiate you from the Real McCoy are the same people who would rather see him dead. And, even more

unfortunately for you, none of those people will have mercy on someone who risks his life for the man that they loathe more than anyone, or anything, else. The fact that you have no choice in the matter, that this life was foisted upon you, is irrelevant to them. None of them would so much as sigh upon learning of your death.

5. Talk little until you have been coached enough to sound like him. It will be strange answering questions with a nod or a smile, but voice and tone are very difficult to mimic. Even if it may seem strange to remain silent when the man that you are portraying is never lacking in something to say, your patience will be important in the long run. And whether he knows it or not, he may win allies who meet you instead of him because they walk away believing that their country's leader is far more agreeable in person than on television after exchanging a few smiles and nods with you.

6. Discover what made him fall in love with his wife. Be good to her in all the ways that he once was, before he realized that he could find anything he wanted in the mistresses lining up to be with him. There will be nights when he will slip off to enjoy a mistress or two. He will not hide it from anyone, not even his wife. Most nights, she will accept it as simply part of her marriage, an annoyance no different than the dirty socks and underwear he leaves strewn across the bedroom floor. Something to be tolerated. Other nights, nights when she has had too much to drink or she is unable to contain her anger, she will look to you, her husband's physical equivalent, for comfort. Be careful—you may not refuse

any of her advances, but you may also never allow him to find out. The fact that his wife is unfaithful to him will be irrelevant, but anything that tarnishes his reputation or embarrasses him is dangerous. He may not go so far as to have you killed because he still needs you, but he will find any excuse to "travel" to all the least hospitable parts of his country, thereby stripping away any ounce of comfort you enjoy as part of your role.

7. Do not bother trying to win over his children. They will never accept you. When their time comes, because the man you have been charged with impersonating is dead, you may as well be dead too. If one of his opponents, convinced that his death is but a rumour and that he still lives, pulling strings from the shadows, does not kill you after seeing you in the streets in normal clothing, then you will die of poverty, having not received a salary for any of your work. The man you are impersonating and his inner circle will believe that service to your country and its father is payment enough. Upon his death and the ascendance of his heir, you will be cast into the streets, where you will be forced to beg for food. Few will give you anything—the transition period between dictators, even in a simple succession rather than by revolution, is often a sparse time for all.

8. Accept that any injuries that happen to him will have to "happen" to you. Any bullet wounds, any scars resulting from unsuccessful knife attacks—these wounds and battle scars will all need to be visible on your body as well to avoid any deviation from the appearance of your noble

leader. In those moments, remind yourself that pain is merely a part of life.

9. But it is not reciprocal—be careful not to develop any visible scars or blemishes of your own. Anything that would make the two of you look different could result in your immediate firing. And, as you well know, being fired from his service often means the firing squad. For that reason, let your vanity take hold, vanity that is directed at looking exactly like him.

10. Train yourself so that each morning, when you wake up, you immediately assume the appropriate role. Most of the time, you will be able to wake up as yourself. You will wake up alone, able to look around and take in the extravagant surroundings before you must collect your thoughts and drape his persona over your own. When you wake up next to his wife, it will be the same—she knows exactly who you are, and to act as him would be ridiculous, even mocking. There will be other times, however, when you will wake up next to one of his mistresses, one of the few he allows you to dabble with, or one he no longer has any use for (steer clear of his favorites, lest you find your head on a pike). Those mornings, compose yourself in order to keep the mystery alive. She may suspect that you are not him, but so long as you do not come right out and say anything, she will not be certain (and she will not say anything, knowing full well that if she did and was wrong, it may be one of the last things she ever said). This mystery, and the accompanying uncertainty, will enhance the encounter,

maybe even give you something to laugh about once she has left.

11. If you have done everything right, the day that he is finally killed—and he will be—if they look at his heir as a monster—which they will—and if there is an opportunity to exalt you, his wife and all of those around will install you in his place. They will brush aside any accusations that you are not the real one and swear that all along, you were the original and that he was the double. And in so many ways, if you have done everything as advised, it will be true.

The Dictator

There was once a dictator who cringed every time he saw someone of his profession fire a gun up into the air. It would be one thing if these dictators were on a farm—purchased with stolen and embezzled funds, of course—in the middle of a deserted countryside, but these men had the habit of firing their pistols up in the air during speeches and rallies in front of thousands of people. Whenever he saw it happen, he wanted to reach through his television set and wring the neck of the perpetrator. Like every child, this dictator was taught that what goes up must come down, and so whenever he saw the smoke from a loaded pistol on television, he wondered where that bullet—flying up through the air, only to come back down at an acceleration of ten meters per second— would land. Would it land safely without harming a single soul, or would it come down right on top of an unsuspecting victim?

Movies and other media always portrayed fictional dictators who laughed and waved their guns around, never taking into account the danger in which their actions placed their citizens. But maybe movies were right in portraying dictators as reckless individuals who cared nothing for their people. What were one or two lives compared to the emotional rush you could get screaming slogans for the party line while firing off a round or two, people cheering you on? But this particular man was an idealist in that he still thought that the very word, his professional title—dictator—could be saved from its tarnished place as one of the most malevolent forms of government in a world where democracy was (he could admit) the hot political ideology of the day.

He leaned back on his leather couch and played with the gold buttons on his navy army jacket. His profession dictated the necessity of wearing military regalia regardless of whether or not one had served in the army. Luckily for him, he had been an infantryman for two years before a gunshot wound to his right thigh left him unable to fight, something he often pointed out when people criticized him for not fighting on the front lines during the revolution. The dictator looked down at the single medal on his chest, the one given to him out of pity for his injury. He refused to decorate himself with fake awards and medals the way most other dictators did. How on Earth could his profession earn any sort of respectability if people kept giving bad speeches, wearing medals they did not earn, and shooting guns off into the air irresponsibly? Even if the bullets landed safely in the ground, he was sure that the noise alone was loud enough to damage the hearing of those within a few meters, meaning that the dictator himself would go deaf after a few years in power (unless he was overthrown and killed in brutal fashion, something that seemed to be a common form of termination).

"Sir, they're ready for you."

The dictator looked up at his most trusted assistant. Manuel was also wearing a navy army jacket, but without any medals. At some point during the dictator's rule, the people around him started stripping their uniforms of their medals because they felt that it was not right to be more highly decorated than their chief. What annoyed the dictator to no end was that their medals had been earned—won for truly heroic deeds that needed to be remembered. Manuel had twelve honors alone, most of which he had earned for bravery on the front lines, and yet he hid them away in a shoebox as if they were dirty magazines that were soiled with use. Whenever the dictator asked his advisers why none of them wore their medals, they did not give him a straight answer, but instead chose to shrug their shoulders, look down at their feet, or change the subject.

The dictator turned off the television and stood up. He picked up the two guns that he always carried on his person: a loaded pistol strapped to the inside of his jacket, which he had carried since his scant soldiering days, and a cap gun housed in a belt holster, which he used during his speeches. He may not have approved of firing bullets up in the air, but he understood the dramatic value of being able to emphasize each phrase with a loud bang. With his low booming voice and firearm theatrics, he had been able to stay in power through his speeches and television addresses and had relied very little on terror and violence to keep his people in check for the past two decades.

Unfortunately, regardless of how prosperous his country became, people on the outside, with their fancy educations and fancy diction, always condemned him for not doing things the right way, the democratic way. He had hoped democracy would be another of the trendy political ideologies that would eventually be proven wrong, like communism or fascism. But one by one, other dictators who subscribed to everything but democracy would fail miserably and end up in a jail for their abuses of power. Whenever he was asked what he believed in, he tried his best to avoid attaching his name to any "ism," and instead filled most interviews with descriptions of the things he wanted for his country—the end of poverty, respect from other nations, and a booming economy—things that almost every ideology desired.

Regardless of what he did or did not say, he was inevitably painted in a negative light. In the past few months, more and more problems arose—a drought that wiped out most of the year's bean crop, an impending war with a nation who enjoyed flexing her muscle, and trade barriers sprouting all over the place. The country would dissolve if something drastic did not happen.

"They've been chanting your name for the past few hours. They want to know what you are going to do." Manuel pulled aside part of the large red curtain and looked out at the thousands of people cramming the square.

"It would be better if they wished me dead," the dictator responded.

Manuel let the curtain drop. "Maybe it's finally our time."

The dictator nodded. "Maybe this is why they put all of my kind in jail. We don't get out when we have the chance."

He lay his hand on the gold doorknob and winked at his comrade. "It's time."

When the dictator stepped outside, cheers and the rattle of gunfire immediately greeted him. He shook his head slowly in the hopes that the bullets would land safely in the ground. If any casualties were to take place, there would be yet another incident used against him in the democratic newspapers.

He raised his hand. A hush fell over the crowd. He reached into his pocket and pulled out the pieces of paper where he had scribbled a speech that he thought would buy him a few more months to try to save his country.

A few more gunshots rang out and he dropped the pieces of paper onto the white stone beneath his feet. He wondered if the people even paid attention to the things he said. He knew that if the positions were reversed and he was the one starving in the streets, he would have much better things to do with his day than listen to an antiquated dictator on his last legs.

And then it dawned on him. It seemed the obvious choice, the only way to go out on top and give his country a chance—the outside world would take notice and start sending aid for his people.

The dictator reached inside his military jacket and pulled out his revolver. He looked up into the sky and smiled. He raised the gun into the air, and as he did, he felt the direction of the wind as it blew against his fingers. He had always been a great physics student. *Objects do not behave as they do in a vacuum,* he reminded himself.

"For liberty and for God," he shouted. He pulled the trigger of his revolver. Cheers erupted from the crowd. He hoped God heard his prayers and would help guide the speeding bullet upwards until its peak and then ensure that its downward trajectory would help him overcome the one billion-to-one odds. He hoped his calculations were correct. Already he could feel the bullet strike his own head, and he smiled, and held tightly to the single medal on his chest.

The Jesus Fish

When she woke up to feed her three goldfish—Onegin, Chomsky, and Bert—her heart sank as she noticed Onegin floating on the surface of the filthy green water. She called her roommate for help, to no avail. Of course Tara would not be there. It was Sunday morning and she had spent her night drinking concoctions as dark and green as the algae-infested water that their three babies inhabited. When she looked into the aquarium, through the absinthe green, she prepared for the worst, wondering whether the other two were moments from death as well. But there they were, Chomsky and Bert, swimming around, their short-term memories already forgetting that their twosome was once a threesome. She took a small Ziploc bag and a soup spoon and went to scoop up the once-hardiest of her fish; only, as the spoon made contact with his body, Onegin turned over and swam away, meeting for the thousandth first time his two aquarium buddies. In that moment of recognition, she renamed him Jesus, but not with the hard "J" sound, but rather the softer Spanish one, said in the exact same way as when she witnessed the miraculous event and whispered a soft breathless prayer.

Cedrick Mendoza-Tolentino

That Wedding Dress

She bought it used from the Housing Works just south of Houston, where it had hung for four months on a metal bar with other discarded ones. Most of them had a yellow tint, including the one that she eventually purchased and walked with down the aisle. He had not noticed any discoloration as he danced with her in front of all their friends and loved ones, though his mother, traditional as always, wondered why his son would have chosen one of *those* girls, too silly to save it til marriage. As people told her how beautiful she looked, she could not help but wonder if they were mocking her behind her back, wondering why she was so poor that she could not have gotten a new dress. Later that night, while he kissed her neck, she could not take her eyes off the yellow-tinted dress lying at her feet. She wondered what had happened to the person the dress was made for: the one that had actually agonized over different styles, selected this one, and then waited for months, eager to have it fit her body perfectly. As he slid his fingers gently over her bare skin, her mind wandered through question after question. Did that woman no longer love her husband? Was the divorce so ugly that she could no longer bear to have that dress in her possession? As he slowly guided her to his—now, their—bed, she was struck by this sudden fear that, like the dress's previous owner, maybe she had made a mistake, too. And in the moments before she closed her eyes and decided to worry about these things another day, she wondered how long it would be before someone else felt the dress against her skin. Because if the dress at the foot of their bed was ever to be worn again, it would not be by her.

Mikhail

Betsy loved the way Mikhail's lips felts against hers. The only other men—boys, really—she had kissed were too forceful, too eager to get to first base. Mikhail never forced her to do anything, never tried to force his tongue down her throat the way a more inexperienced man would have. Some people would have complained about how cold and stiff his lips were, or how he always smelled like paraformaldehyde.

"Betsy, what are you doing here so late?" Amanda, another medical student, asked.

"Oh, nothing." Betsy threw the plastic sheet back over Mikhail's body.

"I can't believe you're still here. The anatomy midterm isn't for another three weeks. Don't tell me you've already started studying."

Betsy wiped her lips with the back of her hand. "Yeah, I just wanted to get an early start. Dr. Stevenson said the midterm might be cumulative, and I don't remember anything in the digestive tract."

"Please. We all know you got the highest grade in anatomy last semester. You spend more time here than anyone else in the school. You spend more time here than in our apartment."

Betsy shrugged. "I don't know. I guess I'm just really interested in this stuff."

"Well, that's why you want to be a doctor." Amanda took a black hairband out of her purse and pulled her hair into a ponytail. "Well, that Atul Gawunde reading is finishing up soon, and I told Alexis and Mark I'd meet them at the Heights for drinks. You want to join us?"

"It's okay. I'm kind of tired. I think I'll just finish up here and then head home."

"You sure? Nicholas is going to be there. You know he's had a crush on you for ages, right?"

Betsy looked down at Mikhail. "I really want to finish this stuff up."

"Okay. Well, don't wait up for me. I might stay over at Mark's tonight."

Betsy exhaled as she watched her roommate leave. There had been a number of close calls, but most people assumed she just really liked anatomy. She pulled the plastic sheet back and looked down at Mikhail, the cadaver she had been assigned at the start of the semester. She ran the back of her hand along his cheek, glad that she was not at one of the medical schools that had such few resources that they had to assign multiple people to a cadaver. Betsy was glad Mikhail was hers and hers alone.

Ever since her first boyfriend James had almost raped her their junior year of high school, Betsy had a terrible streak with boys. For whatever reason, she attracted guys who thought that it was only a matter of time before "no" became a "yes." After her last boyfriend slapped her and called her a tease, she had given up on finding the right guy. That is, until she found Mikhail.

One of the socks that covered his hands fell gently to the ground. Betsy picked up the blue and red argyle sock and gently placed it back over Mikhail's right hand. Each person had been given a pair of white socks to place over their cadaver's hands, but Betsy thought Mikhail deserved something better. She went out and bought some fashionable socks, ones that she thought Mikhail would have worn if he were alive. Most people thought it was cute, but others laughed and snickered when her back was turned.

The socks were used because the hands were one of the last things dissected and needed to be protected. The nerves were some of the smallest and most delicate, which meant they were better saved for later, when first-year medical students were more skilled with a scalpel and forceps.

She knew that her infatuation was weird, but she didn't care. She always spent most of her time alone, and this way she felt she was almost being more social than normal. There were only 6 more weeks left in the semester, so all of this would be coming to an end, but in many ways, Betsy thought of this as the longest, healthiest relationship she had ever been in. Thanks to Mikhail and his body, she had gotten an A in the class.

Betsy kissed Mikhail's cheek, closing her eyes and taking the time to enjoy the feel of her lips against his cold skin.

Unlike her classmates, she enjoyed the smell of the anatomy lab, and did not mind the way her clothing and hair smelled for hours after class. In many ways, Betsy thought she was more prepared than her classmates for having a strong smell follow her around. She had been a swimmer in high school and college, so the smell of chlorine, not as strong as paraformaldehyde, had permeated from her hair and skin wherever she went.

"Hey, what are you doing?

Betsy's head flew up. "Oh, you scared me Arthur."

"Were you smelling your cadaver?"

"No." Betsy's stomach dropped.

Arthur, one of the teaching assistants, walked over and sat down on one of the metal stools. "Didn't want to go to the Gawunde talk?"

Betsy shook her head. Both her hands were clenched into fists under the table. "You neither?"

"No. I don't like his writing. I wanted the night to catch up on some reading."

"Yeah, I wanted to review before we moved on." Betsy picked up a pair of rat-toothed forceps and picked at some loose tissue around Mikhail's exposed heart.

Arthur picked up a probe from Betsy's tray and pressed Mikhail's heart gently. "This guy was either an incredible athlete or suffered from extensive hypertension. Look at the size of his heart muscle."

"I think he must have been an athlete." Betsy gestured to Mikhail's legs. A large flap of skin hung loosely near his calf. "His leg muscles are huge."

"Yeah, he looks well built. I wonder how he ended up here."

Betsy picked at a small deposit of fat above Mikhail's heart. "I have no idea."

Arthur put the probe down. "Well, tomorrow is going to be an exciting day. You guys are going to start dissecting the face."

Betsy mistakenly dropped the forceps and looked down at her feet. "Really? I thought we were going to spend more time on the lower extremities."

Arthur shook his head. "No. Dr. Stevenson says you've fallen behind some of the other sections and it's time to catch up. Don't worry. If you feel like we're going too fast, there will be review sessions at the end of the semester.

"That's great." Betsy tried to muster as much enthusiasm as she could. She thought she had more time before having to dissect Mikhail's face. Much more time.

"Well, a lot of students find that dissecting the face is the toughest. I think when you dissect the rest of the body, none of it seems real. But when you cut into the face, that's when you start to realize this guy once had a soul."

"I guess." Betsy blinked quickly to hold back some tears. "I never thought about it like that."

Arthur stood up and smiled. "Don't worry. Some day, you'll be operating on real people. That'll be much better.

Anyways, I'm going to head back to the library to finish some reading. But if you get the chance, read the chapter about the optic nerve. If you work really quickly, you might get to that tomorrow." Arthur waved and walked out of the lab.

Betsy felt a tear run down her cheek. She ran her hand along Mikhail's face, sad that it would be the last time she would get to see it in its natural state. She had an intense urge to take the scalpel and cut off his lips. Maybe she could store them somewhere. She thought about how easy it would be to simply take a saw and cut off Mikhail's head, maybe hide it in her room somewhere. But she knew it wouldn't be the same.

Betsy pushed Mikhail to one side of the metal table and sat down beside him. She knew that if anyone came by and saw what she was doing, she would never hear the end of it. She thought she may even have to go to psych services or talk to the dean. But she didn't care. It was the last night she would get to see and feel Mikhail's face. Betsy swung her legs up onto the table. She adjusted the plastic sheet so that everything but his face was covered, and pressed her body next to his. She kissed his cheek and laid her head against his, knowing she would never be able to do this again.

"I'll miss you," Betsy said, letting the smell of paraformaldehyde fill her lungs. She closed her eyes and fell asleep.

Teddy

You will get a letter tomorrow that will arrive in a flat cardboard mailer. Do not, I repeat, do not bend it. Before you open it, make sure you have a pencil and an eraser. Not a mechanical one, but a soft wooden one. Make sure the tip is not too sharp—you do not want to damage the paper inside. Carefully open the envelope and lay the single piece of paper on a flat surface.

You will see, on that sheet of plain, 8.5 x 11 white paper, a bear. He may be smiling. He may be asleep. Whatever you do, do not scare him. When he sees you, he is likely to curl into a ball and cover his head with his paws. This is important: the first words out of your mouth must be given in a whisper because he has never heard a human voice before, and his ears need time to adjust. He has never used them before. Speak softly and slowly. Draw a box around him because he will likely start running. If he makes it to the edge of the page and runs off, he will be lost to you forever. He does not know that, but it is one of the many things you will have to teach him.

Introduce yourself. Do not make any sudden movements with your hands. He will likely be crying and scratching at the box around him. Anything you draw on the page is as real to him as the pencil in your hand is to you. You do not have to be an artist. Draw everything as best you can. The key is to imagine exactly what you want to draw in your mind, complete with taste, texture, and smell. If you let the image slip from your mind, if you let the jar of honey you drew turn into an angry bee, your bear will be covered in bee stings in a matter of moments. This will take practice, but in time, you will be able to conjure up anything for your bear with a few lines and simple shapes.

The first thing you draw will be important: make it small and simple. Anything too complex will confuse him, maybe scare him. If you scare him now, it will take you weeks to get him comfortable enough to uncurl out of his ball when you are in the room.

When he sees what you have drawn, it will take a few moments for him to uncurl himself and start inspecting the object. He'll likely sniff and poke it with his paws. Do not make any sudden movements while he does this. If he likes it, draw him another one. If not, try something else. Whatever it is, draw it slowly so he can connect the object and pencil to you. Once you have drawn the second object, smile at him, introduce yourself, and then leave him alone for a few hours.

Come back late at night when he is likely to be asleep. Gently erase the box you drew around him and draw a border around the page as close to the edge as you can to give him space to roam. Draw him a big breakfast and something to play with. In our experience, the bears love big rubber balls. That will keep him entertained for weeks, maybe even months.

Set up a schedule for the next few days. Take some time off work and be prepared to spend several hours with him each day. During this initial period, research what kinds of foods bears eat, and provide an ample supply. Also feel free to draw some of your favorite foods: pizza, ice cream, chocolate—whatever you enjoy. He'll like them too. But remember, this is only in addition to his normal food. He will get sick if his diet consists only of human foods.

Once you have gotten through these initial days, ease him into a routine. Feed him at the same time every day. Spend a part of the day reading him a story. Play with him every night. With every passing day, you'll start to notice that he will look at you with warmth and love. He'll be sad when you leave for work each day and overjoyed every time he sees you.

Draw him anything your imagination can think of: a big house, or cave full of cushions and rubber balls to play with, or a jungle gym. Avoid anything involving rope or things he can hurt himself with. And remember, always draw the things softly, careful not to damage the paper. If by some chance you poke a hole or tear the page, make sure to draw a box around it immediately in case he slips and falls off the page.

Years will pass and your friendship will grow. He will be more loyal to you than anyone you will ever know. While you grow older, his appearance will remain exactly the same. You may be tempted to share him with others, but be careful with who you ultimately entrust. They may not understand what is going on and do something stupid. The last thing you want is to have him stolen away from you, which has happened before. Just be careful.

There will soon come a time when you sit down to write a will. Here is where things get tricky. Death can come suddenly or be a prolonged process. If there comes a time when you realize your death is approaching, sit down with him and explain what is happening. It will be hard. He won't understand at all. But be patient and explain fully what is happening. Then comes the hardest part of all: take an eraser and erase the border you made around the page. Explain to him that there is a world for him beyond the page and that it is time for him to move on. That there are others waiting for him. But the unfortunate could happen—you could die before having the chance to explain these things to him, so you must leave crystal-clear instructions in your will to the person you trust most in the world. He was made for you and you alone and no other person can take care of him. Your instructions must clearly explain that he or she cannot keep him and must erase the border and find a way to coax him off the page.

That is everything you need to know. Take good care of Teddy. In many ways, he was meant to care for you.

The Food Truck Owner

You sit with your back against the bronze statue of Ken Kesey in the square bearing his name, a box of Voodoo Doughnut between your feet and an aluminum baseball bat leaning against the inside of your right leg. You are wearing an Oregon Ducks hat tucked low, but you needn't worry. It's so dark that even with the soft warm glow of the streetlamps, someone could be a few feet away and not even notice you are there.

As you reach into the box and pull out a Bacon Maple Bar doughnut, a soft mist starts to fall. You chuckle, thinking back to when you first moved to Eugene, when you popped open your umbrella whenever it misted. Most took you for a PhD student at the University of Oregon or a tourist, though most tourists were there to visit the university for one reason or another. Now, a year later, the umbrella stayed home unless a heavy downpour was in the forecast, which was rare, if ever.

Minutes pass, and you wonder whether your waiting will be in vain, that you are no different than Vladimir and Estragon waiting for Godot. At least those two had each other. All you have is a bronze statue. Then again, as you bite into a second doughnut—this, a raspberry-filled concoction—you are better off than those two. They didn't have doughnuts.

As a budding restaurateur yourself, you wished you had been the one who brought these doughnuts to Eugene. Instead, you brought Komic-Kati, a food truck—more food cart, given that it had no wheels—that combined Kati rolls and comic books. The combination had been a hit in Eugene, a city where people liked their bars stocked full of arcade games. It probably also helped being located a few feet from Voodoo Doughnuts, so that people could grab one of your snacks before grabbing a doughnut and chocolate milk.

Your success, unfortunately, came with some unwanted attention. At night, the large crowds that lined up for your food during the day were replaced by the many homeless that called Eugene home. That attention, in and of itself, was fine, and you enjoyed giving away any leftover food after closing up for the night. It saved you from having to throw it away. That generosity, however, soon caught the attention of a pair of would-be thugs who wanted more than your leftovers. When you refused their offer of protection in exchange for a small fee—which two other food cart owners agreed to pay—you showed up the next day to the windows of your food cart shattered. When they returned that evening, they once again offered their "protection" from the "vagabonds" that would do such a thing. You refused.

"I'm trying to run a business. Come on."

"Well, we're running a business too."

The next few mornings, you're greeted with more damage to your cart. The police were of little help, saying there was insufficient evidence and that they lacked the resources to monitor the cart all evening. It didn't matter—

this wasn't the first time you had had this problem. In New York, some local toughs had sought money from you in exchange for "protecting" your bar. Like everyone in the neighborhood, you acquiesced, until their demands grew so great that you could either pay up or close up. You dealt with them the same way you planned to deal with these two: with the large end of a baseball bat.

There was a reason why you had left New York shortly thereafter.

When you hear their voices, it's confirmation that you won't, in fact, be waiting endlessly like Vladimir and Estragon. They pass by you and stop in front of Komic-Kati, unaware of your presence until you stand and clear your throat. Doughnut crumbs fall to the ground.

"What do we have here?"

"Looks like a man with a bat."

"And a box of doughnuts. Any left for us? Wouldn't mind a roll either."

"Sorry, I'm closed for the night," you say.

"Are you sure?" one says, taking two steps towards you.

You smile before hitting the closer of the two in the head with the bat. He crumples to the ground. Before the second can escape, you take his knees out from under him.

"Are you crazy? We're going to kill you. I'm going to kill you."

"I highly doubt that," you say as you bring the bat above your head. "I highly doubt that."

In Character

In preparation for your summer job at Six Flags Great Adventure as one of the many tasked with wandering the grounds dressed as a superhero or cartoon character, you decide to rent a Batman costume and wander New York to get "in character." It is an exercise inspired by Mr. Greenberg, your eleventh-grade math teacher and director of the annual school play, who asks all his performers to do the same.

"Until you can no longer distinguish between yourself and your role, you will never be able to fully realize your character on stage."

While most treated the exercise as a joke, you took it very seriously. It was only because of the seriousness with which you approached this exercise that you were able to do justice to your last two roles: Pirate Number 6 in *Peter Pan* and Hyena Number 2 in *The Lion King*. Mr. Greenberg said that of all his students, past and present, only you could take an ensemble part and turn it into the star of the show (you hope, however, that next year he will cast you as a lead so that you will not have to steal the spotlight from those who it was actually meant for). You know that if you can bring that seriousness to your summer job, you could be the best Batman Six Flags has ever seen.

Once you put on the suit, which you rented from a cheap costume shop in Union Square—the low prices were obviously possible because they did not clean their costumes between rentals—you realize you do not know which Batman you should be. The costume may have been the modern Christian Bale version, but you wonder if that is too dark for children. You believe something in-between Adam West and Michael Keaton's portrayals would work but are uncertain (especially because your primary audience will not be old enough to know who they are).

When you call and present the problem to Mr. Greenberg, he is glad that you continue to use his time-honored acting technique. However, he throws a wrench in it all: "Are you in fact meant to be portraying Batman or an amusement park employee portraying Batman? Before you dismiss me out of hand, ask yourself: Is there any scenario where Batman would find himself pandering to a bunch of children in an amusement park?"

Mr. Greenberg abruptly hangs up and leaves you to ponder his query. The more you think about it, the more you realize that while you *should* be visualizing a high school student dressed as Batman (in other words, yourself), you did not spend $200 to be yourself dressed up as Batman. You want to *be* Batman. And so, when you spend your first few days wandering New York, it is as Bruce Wayne beneath the Batman costume. You do your best to move stealthily through the streets, ducking into alleyways when you can and practicing taking on and off the suit at a moment's notice. The evenings are the hardest, as drunk college students had no problems harassing the guy wearing the Batman costume. No wonder Batman chose to lurk in the shadows and travel along rooftops.

After a few days of mixed results, you realize where you should have gone from the start: Times Square. What better place to get the experience needed than somewhere full of other costumed folk looking to make money off of tourists?

The next morning, within minutes of exiting the subway at 42nd St., you are mobbed by a brother and sister who want nothing more that to have their picture taken punching the Dark Knight. After standing in various poses, you understand why so many donning costumes in Times Square insisted on being paid: It's hard work. Between the cost of renting the costumes and the patience needed to deal with children, you cannot imagine what kind of person would put on an Elmo costume and do this (or the kind of people who would do it that did not belong in jail).

You continue the afternoon wandering around with the others in costume, posing for pictures and waving at tourists. It is easy to identify the New Yorkers—they barely register your existence and, when they do, they look at you as if you are a nuisance that needs to stop clogging the sidewalk.

But when the clock hits 3 p.m., the time you have set to take a break, get some coffee, and recharge—you assume that Batman must drink loads of coffee in order to spend his days as Bruce Wayne and his evenings breaking kneecaps—you notice one of the three Elmos you have spent the day with grabbing at a woman's purse. In that moment, you realize that your brief time spent as Batman has gotten you ready for moments like this. You react just as Batman would—you spring into action and jump Elmo.

A few hours later, while sitting in jail as you await your parents and their inevitable lectures, you pray that your actions will not jeopardize your summer job. In those brief moments, when you were raining punches down on a defenseless Elmo, you knew you had truly become Batman. The kids visiting Six Flags Great Adventure would be in for a real treat.

You do, however, wish you had received some of the specialized training that Bruce Wayne had received. Batman would have never allowed himself to be arrested and even if he had, he would never have allowed for his secret identity to be compromised. He would have been devising a plan to get out of jail without a trace.

With all these thoughts racing through your head, you hope that your parents would be arriving soon—you really needed to get back out there to implement your new ideas and fully immerse yourself in the character.

Seeing is Believing

You lean back on the sofa, take a bite of a brownie, and place it back onto the plate alongside a dozen other half-eaten baked goods. The plate is covered by remnants of brownies, cupcakes, and other dessert items with different-colored frosting. Your six-year-old son Trevor decided just that morning that Santa must be tired of going from house to house and eating the same cookies over and over again. It would be up to the two of you, he declared, to provide some variety to Santa's diet. Luckily for you, the local bakery was open until noon today, before everyone headed home to celebrate the holiday. Also, luckily for you, the bakery had not been cleaned out by all the people smart enough to reserve their cakes and desserts ahead of time or all of the people smart enough not to get to the bakery 15 minutes before it closed.

You pick up a glass of room-temperature milk and drink half of it in a single gulp. Last year, your husband Michael made the mistake of drinking all of the milk, and the two of you had to listen to your son worry about whether too many bathroom breaks would prevent Santa from delivering all of his presents in time. Trevor's letter to Santa this year, which is currently sitting in your office, asked Santa if he had a bathroom on his sleigh. Santa's response, written on a small index card that you left beside the plate of half-eaten baked goods, said Trevor had nothing to worry about—"I only drink a small sip from each household." The note also thanked Trevor for being so thoughtful with the desserts, but also let him know that Oreos were his favorite. This way, next year, all you would have to do is buy Oreos.

Happy with this year's crime scene, you pick up a second glass. This one is filled with Baileys and vodka. You turn on the television and are greeted by Sean T telling you that if you did *Insanity* for 60 days, the things that would happen to your body would be "insane." If Michael were still around, he would have picked up his shirt and showed you his belly. He would have asked if you still thought he was sexy (You loved him for many things, but his "sexiness" had never been one of them).

You have never been a heavy drinker, so the alcohol hits you quickly. Ever since Michael died, you have found yourself drinking more, but not so much that you would consider yourself an alcoholic. You close your eyes and enjoy the throbbing sensation as someone shares how *Insanity* helped her lose 35 pounds.

"Try *Insanity* now, risk-free for 30 days. If you're not satisfied, send it back for a full refund."

You bolt awake, wondering how long you have been out. The clock says 4:46 a.m. You would have to get to bed soon if you want to be able to get up when Trevor inevitably barges into your bedroom, eager to open his presents. You turn off the television. "No matter what I do, I'll never look like that," you say.

"Mommy?"

You spin around, almost knocking the glass of Baileys from the coffee table. "Hey there. What are you doing awake?"

Trevor jumps onto the couch. "Who were you talking to?" His eyes settle on the plate of half-eaten desserts. "Santa? Santa?" He jumps off the couch and looks at the boxes of presents under the tree. He then runs to the window and looks up into the sky. "I can't believe you never told me you knew him."

You look at your son and then back at the Christmas tree and smile. "Sometimes I can't believe it myself, kiddo. Come on," you say, grabbing his arm and guiding him back to his bedroom. "I'll tell you all about it in the morning when we open up your presents."

A Former Child Star's Fall From Grace

He regretted making the sex tape with that senator's daughter. It had happened in a hotel room just off the Vegas Strip. She was there for a bachelorette party for one of her sorority sisters—how cliché—and had absolutely freaked out when she saw him drinking alone at the hotel bar (in the bride-to-be's defense, she had wanted to do a quiet weekend at her family's cabin in Maine, but was quickly shot down by everyone in her bridal party who wanted an excuse to relive their so-called college glory days). He imagined that these kinds of occurrences were common for Justin Bieber or those guys from One Direction, but for him, it had been over a decade since people had flocked to see him (and at that time, he had been much too young to truly take advantage of, or know what to do with, all of that particular type of attention). While he felt rather embarrassed when all eyes in the bar turned to him and his rabid fan, deep down he was extremely flattered and grateful for the attention.

"Oh my God! I used to have a *Tiger Beat* poster of you in my bedroom!"

"Poster? How would you like to have the real thing instead?" No one had ever said he was the smoothest talker, but he had never needed to be.

When the sex tape was released three weeks later, he wanted to find a lawyer and sue Apple right away. He had thought that anything stored on Apple's iCloud would be safe after the last major hack had resulted in a number of nude photos of A-List actresses hitting the internet. It was not that he regretted making the sex tape—he was rather proud of his performance. It was that he regretted making the sex tape with some senator's daughter instead of an actress or reality star perpetually in the tabloids like Lindsay Lohan or Paris Hilton. Maybe then a sex tape, instead of solely being a source of ridicule and embarrassment, would have given him the publicity he needed to get back into the spotlight. Maybe that would have helped him shed the dreaded "Child Actor" label that his agent and seemingly every producer in Hollywood had taught him to loathe. He had been anything but a child in that video.

As he filled every tabloid headline, he regretted not listening to Jodie Foster at last year's Oscars. She had urged him to take some time away from the spotlight, maybe go to college or travel. He had starred in a few box office bombs, and producers were wondering whether he could carry a movie. But taking a break was the last thing he wanted to do. It did not matter that Jodie Foster promised him a role in her next movie if he took a break, the kind of role, she promised, for which actors waited a lifetime. Hollywood was littered with actors and actresses who simply disappeared. He had no interest in being the next Macaulay Culkin. And besides, why should he have listened to her anyways? By the time he was 12, he had already won two Oscars, the same number Jodie Foster had, and he had not needed a degree from Yale to win them (he doubted that even with his two Oscars that Yale or any other prestigious school would have admitted him, given that his SAT scores were so low that his agent once joked that he must have misspelled his name).

He was even more regretful when he watched Jodie Foster thank the Academy when her next film won Best Picture at the Academy Awards a few years later. He would have been happy for her and the kindness she had shown him if not for the fact that Macaulay Culkin had been the one to listen to her and had earned himself a Best Supporting Actor Oscar for the role that was meant for him. It was hard for him to accept that the *Home Alone* kid was the one that had stolen his path to redemption.

His agent had been furious when the sex tape leaked. And his agent had been furious for the same reason he had been.

"Seriously? You couldn't have done it with some washed-up actress or pop star? I could have spun this with just about any whiny B-Lister, but a senator's daughter? *That* senator's daughter? Sometimes, I wonder whether I should have gone with that other kid in the Pampers' commercial instead of you."

He tuned out the rest of the lecture, as he was used to dealing with his agent's frustrations. Just two weeks before the sex tape leaked, he had had to sit through a similar lecture from his agent after a disastrous performance on *Celebrity Jeopardy!* had resulted in the producers of *The Bachelor* deciding that he was not quite right for the show. Apparently, those producers did not think audiences would be enamoured with a guy who thought that Boston was the capital of the state of New England and that the sum of the angles of a circle was 180 degrees. Those producers did not seem to think having a six-pack and a winning smile were enough.

"Stop, just stop it. If there's nothing you can do about this, then you're fired. I mean, if Kim Kardashian and Paris Hilton can turn their sex tapes into millions, why can't I? I'm already famous."

"Hey, if you want to be some laughingstock, sure, I can find you something right now. But you pay me because you still want to be a 'serious actor.' So, you tell me. How am I supposed to convince casting agents that you're the next George Clooney when you're busy doing stupid stuff like this?" my agent yelled.

"Get out. Maybe if I had fired you sooner, I'd have been in *The Lord of the Rings* instead of having to watch it like everyone else in the world!"

As he watched his agent storm off, he thought of the roles he most regretted letting get away, none of which he regretted more than losing a part in *The Lord of the Rings*. At the time, he had not known what a hobbit was and his agent's description—"It's like a short fat elf"—had not made it the most enticing of roles. When he saw pictures of hobbits online, he decided he had no interest in the role. When he saw the movies on the big screen, he had to hold back the tears as he mourned all of the future roles that Elijah Woods and Sean Patrick Astin would be enjoying because they had seen the potential in being a short fat elf when he had not.

In the months after firing his agent, he learned how difficult it was to book roles without one. His name and previous work were not enough. Auditions he thought had gone well were often not even followed up with a courtesy rejection call. The only people who were excited to talk to him were those who ran pornography websites, and that was the last thing he wanted to do. He knew that once he crossed into that world, there would be no going back.

When he did try to find a new agent, it was next to impossible because of his former agent's "exclusive" and "shocking" interview with *Us Weekly* where he called him arrogant, stuck-up, and narcissistic (which should not have been "shocking" because that described almost everyone in Hollywood). If the insults had stopped there, he might have been able to salvage some dignity and convince another agent to give him a shot, but his agent had gone ahead and confirmed the rumours that the reason why he had had not been cast opposite Jennifer Lawrence in the newest Nicholas Sparks movie was because he had terrible breath.

Even two years after the leak, people still associated him with the sex tape more than his Oscar-winning roles. He thought that he would have at least been able to find some small art house film to sign on with, which in turn would convince a young Hollywood executive looking for a good underdog story/person to invest in and give a chance to. Unfortunately, because that damned senator thought that the sex tape was the reason why he was dropped from the short list of next Democratic vice-presidential candidates, the senator had taken it upon himself to ensure that no one hired him for any movies or television shows. He had become something of a Hollywood has-been. Even *TMZ* and the paparazzi stopped caring about where he was at night, which was a bad sign because he had always been a source of good tabloid fodder.

With few places left to go, unless he was prepared to try a "normal" job as a waiter or, God forbid, in retail, he thought that maybe he would try his hand at something he used to mock: infomercials. Inspired by the way that the Academy consistently awarded Oscars to actors and actresses who underwent extreme body transformations, he thought that if he could find an infomercial that showed what he was willing to do to his body for his art, he could convince some Hollywood big wig to give him another chance. He knew there was always a market for infomercials—just look at how famous Shaun T had become by yelling at people to "dig deeper" for his *Insanity* workout. If it meant joining the likes of Charlize Theron and Matt Damon, two who had reaped the benefits Hollywood doled out to those willing to test the limits of their bodies, he was willing to say goodbye to his washboard abs. It was, of course, all in the name of his "art."

Eventually, he managed to convince the creators of the Sculptor, an ab-machine that promised to melt away fat, to use him as their spokesperson. They were shocked at how he had "let himself go," weighing 40 pounds more than he had just a few months before. He promised them that he would do for them what Kirstie Alley had done for Jenny Craig, only in his case, the weight would stay off (he was so confident that he promised to forfeit 50% of his fee if he gained the weight back within 3 years of the first airing of the infomercial). When they agreed, he wanted to jump for joy, knowing that this was the break he was looking for. Hollywood had welcomed Robert Downey Jr. and John Travolta back with open arms. Why not him?

Given his luck, he should have realized that the call he received from the director the night before the first day of filming—consisting of "before" interviews and shots at his new, heavier weight—was not to wish him luck. It had been years since he had been that lucky. Instead, as he listened to the director explain that they had decided to go in a different direction with someone more "real," someone that would be more relatable for the average person, he knew that somehow that senator had gotten to the Sculptor people too.

After thanking the director and hanging up, he sat back on his couch beside what was supposed to be the last Domino's pizza he was ever going to eat. He turned on his television, only to be greeted by an infomercial for skin cream. Before changing the channel, he sighed, looking down at the gut he had developed that peeked out from under his grey t-shirt. He had thought that doing the infomercial would represent the low point of his career before he rose up out of the ashes like a phoenix. Instead, as he cracked open the Domino's box and took a look at the mounds of cheese and pepperoni, he was pretty sure that the low point of his career was still yet to come.

What Lurks Beneath

Every evening, when her daughter asks her to check under the bed for monsters, Penelope has to take a deep breath and steel herself before getting down on her hands and knees to take a look. She never saw anything in the shadows beneath her daughter Lucy's bed. They had moved four times, and in each home, it did not matter—all she found every time she bent down to check were shadows. It did not matter that Penelope never saw anything, she was scared every time her daughter asked her to look. Penelope's fear was so real, so tangible, that every time she did not see anything and then popped up to report that everything was "All clear," the relief on her face was so obvious that it instantly calmed her daughter. Of course, Penelope still had to stay in the room until her daughter fell asleep, just in case she was wrong, but it was never more than a few minutes before Lucy was fast asleep. And every evening, when Penelope gently closed the door behind her, Penelope dreaded knowing that she would have to do it all over again the next night.

Though Penelope's actions may have seemed strange, her fears were not unwarranted. Unlike the millions of children whose fears of what lurked beneath their beds was a product of an overactive imagination fueled by movies and television shows, Penelope had actually seen a monster beneath her own bed. One night, when she was 10 years old, long after her parents had gone to bed, she had awoken to the distinct sound of chewing. When she had gotten out of bed to investigate, a long dark creature poked its head out and smiled. After Penelope screamed, the creature disappeared, but the image was enough to haunt her for the rest of her life.

And so, every night when Penelope checked under the bed for her daughter, she wondered whether she was ever going to see that same monster again. Every night that Penelope did not was a night that she could sleep calmly. So every night when she popped her head up, relieved to find nothing lurking beneath, Penelope knew that not only would she be sleeping soundly that night, her daughter would be too.

Pandora's Box

Before finding a permanent home in a small glass case in The Robert and Renée Belfer Court for Early Greek Art in the Metropolitan Museum of Art, the ancient Greek artifact remained hidden in Lydia Sears' basement for 12 years, nestled between a box of old children's clothing and a long-outdated Epson inkjet printer that should have been donated to Goodwill years before. She had no idea of the item's significance—understandable, given it was not a box at all, but rather a large ceramic jar, no different than any of the other knick knacks and kitschy things she had purchased over the years, convinced that the small pendant or miniature statue she saw was a necessary way to commemorate that particular trip or the emotion she felt at that particular moment.

Lydia had purchased this particular item from an estate sale during her honeymoon. The item's previous owner had amassed a large collection of ancient Greek art, but had died mysteriously, leaving no instructions on how to deal with his estate. His children, wanting to make a quick buck, opened the doors to their late father's home and put everything up for sale. Walking through the cavernous home was like walking through a private museum, the walls covered in tapestries and paintings of all shapes and colors. The shelves overflowed with sculptures and other items that really did look as if they belonged at a museum in glass cases behind velvet ropes. If Lydia had her way, she would not only have purchased as many items as she could have fit into her suitcase, she would have purchased the home as well, turning it into a summer getaway, a place where she and her husband could go to take a break or to rekindle their marriage (which she had heard, no matter how much they loved each other, would wane over time).

"Lydia, you can't be serious? Come on now, just choose one item and then let's get back to the beach. Most of these things aren't real. I'll take you to see the real thing at the Met when we get home."

And that was how Lydia had come to purchase a "wine jar" that, according to the people running the estate sale, "may" have once been owned by Aristotle for the very low price of $545 U.S. dollars. It had taken immense restraint not to buy more items, especially when her husband was not looking, but she knew that it would probably not be a good start to their marriage if she immediately disregarded what he had said (which had only become an issue because she had already mailed back two boxes full of souvenirs). While her husband thought that the wine jar was a colossal waste of money—especially considering that she had already purchased two other wine jars—Lydia thought this particular one was the *perfect* item to commemorate their honeymoon.

The problem, which Lydia only discovered once she returned home, was that she could not open the damn thing. The top was stuck, as if someone wanted to make sure that it could never be opened. Unusable for storing wine or anything else, the item remained on a kitchen shelf amongst her cookie jar collection for years. There it remained until it was packed away, stored, and forgotten during a move.

It was not until a decade later that the item returned to the light of day. Discovered by Lydia's daughter, Rosalyn, the item looked exactly as it did when Lydia had first laid eyes on it. When Lydia saw it, she immediately recalled how much she had spent on it, which was especially embarrassing given that it had been nothing more than a display piece that had been "displayed" in the bottom of a box for all to see.

When Lydia told Rosalyn that the reason why the item had never been used was because no one could open it, Rosalyn laughed, always up for a challenge.

"How hard can it be to get off, Mom?" she asked as she gripped the lid tight. Rosalyn had always prided herself on her grip strength.

And somehow, as if being hidden for years had made the artifact change its mind, all Rosalyn had to do was apply a little pressure and the lid came right off. The moment the lid was off, however, Rosalyn and Lydia knew it had been a mistake to open it.

Unfortunately, by the time they managed to put the lid back on, it was too late.

Everything We Knew About Him Before He Left

The last time that we saw our father, I was 13 and Shea was 9. It was 8:35 a.m. on a Monday morning (or at least that's what I remember it to be). He kissed each of us on the forehead before waving goodbye, the same as he did every morning before going to work. Our mother took us to school like she always did. Neither Shea nor I remember anything about what happened that day, but I imagine that it was no different than any other day at school. It was not until our mother pulled up, in tears, at the end of the day that we realized that something was wrong. Our mother had never picked us up before, nor had we ever seen her cry. That day, the day our father left, was full of many firsts and lasts.

He was a fund manager at Ledgerwood & Ryan, one of those hedge funds that would later go under during the financial crisis. When people asked us what he did, we told them he took other people's money and made them more money so that they could retire early. No one was impressed. We wished he was a police officer or, even better, an actor paid to play a police officer on *Law & Order* or *NYPD Blue*. Neither of us had ever seen an episode of either show—our parents told us we were much too young—but our classmate

Martin Spruce's father had been on both shows. And everyone wanted to be friends with Martin.

Physically, we did not resemble our father at all. Shea and I both looked like our mother, sharing her dark brown hair and olive complexion. Our father towered over all three of us at 6'5" and with his blond hair and freckles, he resembled more surfer than hedge fund manager. And he loved his books. He seemed to love them more than he loved us. It was Shea who noticed that first night that his beloved copies of *The Odyssey* and *The Old Man and the Sea* were gone. His copy of Homer's masterpiece was the same annotated copy that he had been carrying with him since his first year of college; while he had bought his first edition of Hemingway's masterpiece on a street corner for $3 from a bookseller who had no idea what he had. Our mother dismissed the missing books as irrelevant, but it was clear that her words sounded hollow even to her. Those books were two of his most prized possessions, along with a pin that he had received for winning a fourth-grade science fair, and the coat our grandfather had given him for his 27th birthday. She did not cry when we insisted that the books were a sign that he was gone, nor did she cry when we pointed out that the coat and pin were gone from the coat rack too, which we thought strange, given that it was the middle of the summer and people were still sweating while in tank tops and shorts. No, it was not until our mother found his wedding ring on her bedside table that she started to cry once again, realizing that he was indeed gone.

The bedside tables had been his idea. He loved to read late into the night, but our mother liked having him beside her when she went to bed. While her table was almost always empty, his looked as if he had taken a drawer and emptied it out on top—coins, receipts, lint, and an assortment of pens were scattered along the surface, along with a pile of whatever books he was reading at the time. We used to joke with him that he was always starting books, but never finishing them. He would laugh and mess up our hair before going back to whatever book was on his lap. He must have finished them, because the pile on top the bedside table never held the same collection of books for very long.

When I was 5 years old, I was diagnosed with attention deficit disorder. When the doctor told us, my mother looked relieved, as if that explained so much. My father, on the other hand, was beside himself. He thought all of it was a load of nonsense, that of course I had problems focusing on things. I was a child. All children were like that. Even after it was clear that the pills had a positive effect on me, he still insisted that it was all unnecessary. While he had never been religious, our mother was. They often clashed about whether religion was to have an important place in our lives. Whenever she talked about the importance of God and having God in our lives, he would ask her whether God would be happy that she was forcing her son to take pills in order to change who he was. She never responded to that.

I was told that my first word was Dada and Shea's was Mama. I wonder whether I knew what that word meant or whether it was the first time anyone heard me put together two sounds that resembled a word. I would like to think that that was my first word because I knew what it meant, but of course I cannot be sure. My father used to brag to all of his friends that he was my first word and that the only reason why

Shea's was Mama was because our mother repeated the word over and over again so that she was not left out. Our mother wanted to be able to tell her friends that one of her children had made her their first word too.

Most people seemed to like our father more than our mother. He was the social one, the one who enjoyed being out and about, meeting people and making introductions. Our mother was the quiet one, the Yin to his Yang. It was clear that she loved that he was so comfortable in public and he loved the fact that she never competed with him for that spotlight. She was beautiful, which only added to the perfect symmetry they had when out together. It was at home that our father, without an audience to pander to, and our mother, no longer frightened by any stranger's judgmental eyes, would bicker about anything and everything. It was here, especially late into the evening when they both thought that we were asleep, that they let out their frustrations with one another. Neither Shea nor I ever told them that we could hear them arguing, though maybe we should have. Maybe then he would have stayed.

Our mother had long suspected that he was cheating on her, but she had no proof. She wondered whether someone of his seniority level really needed to stay late at work as often as he did. Wasn't that for the juniors at his firm? When he left, all of her fears were confirmed. He had left for another woman. What else could explain him just getting up and disappearing one day?

But none of us were sure, nor would we ever be sure. All we knew for certain was that one day he was with us, and the next day he was gone.

Stains

After inspecting the long white cape, it is clear that Shout's triple-acting formula is steeped in hyperbole: the cleaning agent certainly did not cling, penetrate, and lift away stains. Or at least it did not cling, penetrate, and lift away every stain. Although the Shout had washed away the blood, something that ordinary laundry detergent would have succeeded in doing as well, patches of grease and motor oil remain on the long white cape. You would write to SC Johnson to complain if you thought you would get anything other than a one-sentence apology and a voucher for a free bottle of Shout, the cleaning agent that had failed to clean what you had needed it to. You have no idea how your boss, a guy who could fly and shoot electricity from his fingertips, always came back covered in blood, grease, and motor oil. It was as if someone specifically told him that using superpowers in a fight was dishonourable.

"Niles, I need to leave in twenty minutes. Can you get everything ready by then?" your boss asks over the intercom.

"I'll try my best," you shout, rather than press the intercom button to respond. As you grip the Tide pen, hoping that being the "#1 Instant Stain Remover" actually counted for something, you curse your parents for naming you Niles.

It was as if your parents were tempting fate the way that parents who named their daughter Destiny or Bambi do. From the moment they filled out Niles on your birth certificate, your employment ceiling was psychiatrist and employment floor was butler, along with everyone else named Niles, Jeeves, or Smithers. Your only comfort was that you cleaned up after someone who spent his nights fighting crime instead of some trust-fund brat.

The Tide pen smells horrific, but it appears to be working: the once concentrated black grease and motor oil are now patches of light grey. Someone would have to be standing right next to the cape in a brightly lit room in order to notice anything.

"It looks better, but still not good enough. I can't go to a *GQ* photoshoot dressed in that." Your boss hovers over you, shaking his head. You have long gotten used to him sneaking up on you without a sound, something that only reinforces your disbelief when he returns from patrolling covered in dirt.

"Why don't you use a different cape? You have four brand new ones."

"You know that's my lucky cape. I want the pictures to be perfect."

"Photoshop?"

"Niles, I want the pictures to be authentic. My lucky cape needs to be there."

You look down and sigh. If he really thought that in the post-*TMZ* world anything was not Photoshopped, he was even more naïve than you thought. "Maybe if you started using one of your other capes, you could do something heroic while wearing it like save the president or something. Then you could have a new lucky cape and we could retire this one."

"Why didn't you clean it sooner?"

"Because you asked me to repaint your helmet, remember?" You pick up the small container of red paint and shake it back and forth. "The one you never use?"

"Well, okay. Keep at it. I'm still not ready to retire this guy just yet." He gestures towards his knee, which hovers a few inches from your forehead. "You did a great job patching this up. Other than a few loose threads, it's as good as new."

"That's because those pants are new. I sewed in those extra threads, you dumb fuck. I'm so glad that your superpowers never required you to develop any detective skills," you think to yourself, holding back a snicker. You are lucky that reading minds is not one of his many powers, or else you would have been out of a job long ago (that, or your body would have washed up at Jones Beach minus a limb or two). You watch him float slowly up the stairs back to the main floor of the small brownstone where you assume he will spend a few anxious minutes going over the things he wanted to convey in the *GQ* interview.

Lucky fucking cape? You apply more Tide liquid to the so-called "lucky cape," which is nothing more than a tablecloth cut in half. An actual cape had been too expensive when he started out. Not everyone could magically work a sewing machine like Peter Parker. You are often tempted to ask one of the Italian restaurants along Mulberry how they dealt with food and wine stains. Maybe they had great dry cleaners. Regardless, whenever you brought up using one of the new capes, which happened to be made from a water-resistant, and therefore stain-resistant, material, he always went back to the same old "How can I use anything other than my lucky cape?" Whenever you really pushed, he would remind you that Michael Jordan always wore his University of North Carolina shorts under his Chicago Bulls uniform, as if that justified wearing his lucky cape and only his lucky cape. Your boss may as well have been Linus carrying around his security blanket.

You set the cape down on the ironing board and stretch your arms above your head. While the foul-smelling Tide liquid is drying, you pick up the small red paint can, careful not to spill any on the white cape (it would be ironic if you managed to get the black stains out only to cover the cape in red paint). Gently applying a thin layer of paint on the oversized helmet your boss never wore because it restricted his visibility, you wonder how different your life would be if you were the one with superpowers. You would certainly go out and save people (all that "With great power comes great responsibility" crap having a profound effect on you and every other would-be hero), but you would have also been sure to make money while doing it. Maybe you would do what the NBA had been unwilling to do and turn yourself into a walking billboard. If something did happen to a lucky cape or some other part of your costume, you could simply put a Nike or Gatorade patch over it.

You set the helmet down and pick up the cape. A quick inspection reveals that Tide's claim of "#1 Instant Stain Remover" is well-deserved. Given what you have been able to do, you have clearly earned the title of #1 Butler. You kiss the

Tide pen and lay it on the desk, knowing that SC Johnson would no longer be getting any of your business. And maybe you would be writing them a letter, one that not only pointed out that Shout failed at living up to its promises but that also pointed out that Tide was in fact a much superior cleaning product.

"So, how is it looking? I can reschedule the interview for a hostage situation, but I am sure they will be less understanding about a costume malfunction."

You pat yourself on the back before reaching for the intercom, getting ready to bask in your boss's praise. You know that what you have managed to clean in such a small period of time is nothing short of a miracle. But as you reach down to press the intercom button, you notice that your fingers are covered in red paint. Your heart beats loudly. When you look down, your worst fears are confirmed: though the black stains are gone, the cape is now covered in red fingerprints.

"Niles, really, what's my estimated time of departure?"

You take a few deep breaths before pressing the intercom button, not knowing how he is going to respond. He has been nervous about this interview for weeks, as he thought this would be the break he needed to hit the big time and become an A-list superhero, the kind that could afford to have an army of butlers waiting on him instead of just one. Maybe someone really would find pieces of you washed up on the shores of Jones Beach tomorrow.

"Sir, we've got a little bit of a problem."

"I know. I needed to leave 5 minutes ago. I'm coming down."

All you can do is close your eyes and pray. Hopefully you will wake up tomorrow and give thanks to your boss like so many others, the only difference being you would be thanking him for sparing your life instead of saving it.

What Comes After

After the stroke,

her family hung a chalkboard around her neck, fastened with duct tape and the same twine the family used to pack up old newspapers for recycling. The stroke had robbed her of her ability to speak, other than in moans that made her cringe and shudder, something especially devastating given she had spent much of her life singing. By the time anyone realized that a whiteboard may have been better—lighter, with a smooth slick surface to write on—she had become used to the chalkboard and refused to use anything else. It had been difficult at first, learning to write at such an awkward angle, having to curl her wrist around so that she could write to express herself without having to flip the board over each time or having to lay the chalkboard on a flat surface. A notepad was no better an alternative—paper was too fragile and ripped too easily when pen met paper, the stroke robbing her of fine motor skills and a soft, deft touch. Over time, she became comfortable wearing the chalkboard around her neck, no different and as unobtrusive as the Crucifix her eldest son had worn since his First Communion. Because words, especially long ones, were too time-consuming to write out, she invented a series of symbols and pictures. The irony of those crudely drawn symbols and pictures was not lost on her family, who used to beg her to write thank you notes and wedding invitations in her beautiful calligraphy. When people looked at her and the dusty board, traces of previous messages and symbols still visible in chalk beneath new ones, they wondered whether her mind was still sharp or whether her mind had become as dull as the pieces of chalk she threw to the side once they were too short to grip in her claw-like hands. Her children wondered whether she had become a prisoner in her body, trapped, or whether part of her mind had been wiped as well, leaving only enough for the most basic of bodily functions. The same children who had once looked at her as a queen, often an unfair one whose anger and punishment they felt was doled out arbitrarily, now looked at her with pity, when they could bear to look at her at all.

But when her youngest granddaughter looked at her, she paid no attention to the way that her left arm hung uselessly at her side or the way that the left side of her face drooped just a little more than the right. No, when her youngest granddaughter looked at her, her granddaughter thought she was lost in a beautiful daydream, one she never wanted to end. Curious what could cause someone to smile and look off into space for so long, her granddaughter always wanted to ask what it was she was dreaming about. She never did ask, however, believing that the daydream was too beautiful to disturb.

My First Billion

My father was the first person to realize I was going to be rich, though it was my mother who had the first opportunity to do so—she was the one who stumbled upon me, at the tender age of seven, a bloody mess with pliers and a pile of baby teeth neatly arranged on a paper towel on my lap. When my father burst into my bedroom to see what my mother's wailing was all about, he too was shocked by the grisly scene. But in the 15 minutes it took my mother to search for towels, call 911, call 911 back to say that no ambulance was needed because she was going to take me directly to the hospital herself, and find her car keys, my father had taken a look at the small pile of teeth and then at the $10 bill sitting on my nightstand and realized why I was acting like a kid in need of a serious exorcism—I was in it for the money. My parents had made the mistake of having the "tooth fairy" give me $20 for my first tooth, half of which I had spent on a comic book, a chocolate bar, and a Coke. Knowing that I had been able to buy all of those things and still have enough to do the exact same thing the next day, all I wanted to do was yank my teeth out so I could make some more money.

That was how my love of money began. While other children were focused on what money bought you—toys, candy, tickets to amusement parks—my focus was on the first step, actually acquiring it.

The problem, of course, was finding a way to make money. My dreams were not full of doctor, lawyer, or banker money, the kinds of jobs that provided more than enough money for anyone seeking a comfortable lifestyle. No, I wanted Bill Gates money. I wanted to make the Palace of Versailles look pedestrian and I wanted to be the guy who Goldman Sachs called when they needed a bailout. I wanted to be in the 0.1% of the 0.1% and I wanted to be the first person picketed by Occupy Wall Street when they held their annual Millionaires March. I never deluded myself into thinking that my dreams of wealth were moral or "good" in any way, but I never thought less of myself because of those aspirations. If anything, I felt vindicated at an early age, as I was the one taking jobs around the neighborhood, while everyone else was doing their best to get out of working. While earning money for delivering newspapers or mowing people's lawns was nice, I struggled to see how $100/week was going to get me where I wanted to go.

The answer was handed to me by my tenth grade English teacher Mr. Phen during a class on *The Great Gatsby*—"If any of you want to be really rich, found a religion. There is no better way to make millions than being the head of a religion." I dismissed it as I did everything my teachers told me, because my father had told me from a young age that "Those who can, do; those who can't, teach." I learned later in life that my father drilled that most clichéd of idioms into me because his own father had done it to him, as if repeating the same nonsense to your own children because you heard it from your own parents was as good enough a reason as any. Because of my father's indoctrination, I looked at Mr. Phen as I did all teachers—a source of authority who deserved very little respect because he had been forced to become a "teacher" due to his inability to be a "doer." Mind you, Mr. Phen did not help his cause when at lunch one day he picked up my copy of the first volume of *The Walking Dead*, leafed through it like one would a trashy tabloid, and then threw it back onto the table, exclaiming, "Why do people read this trash?" I wanted to respond that "We read this trash because it's good and Robert Kirkman has made millions because it's so good. That's why they made it into a television show." But instead, I kept my mouth shut and went back to my peanut butter and jelly sandwich and trashy book full of images of people killing zombies.

I spent the next few years of high school and college doing what any other aspiring multi-billionaire did—I learned how to program and spent endless hours creating games and apps that I thought would help me rise to Mark Zuckerberg fame. Alas, that path was being followed by so many others that by the time I got to college, being That Programming Guy or That App Guy made me one of many instead of a unique individual. The major problem was that I could not come up with an idea that would get me $50,000 a day like the guy who invented Flappy Bird (why he pulled that game off the iTunes Store is beyond me, though I suspect it was because some video game company named Nintendo wrote him a cease-and-desist letter for copying their images. Maybe you've heard of it?).

And then, in the middle of a world religions class, as if my dearly departed teacher Mr. Phen was wondering from his grave why on Earth I had not taken the hint that he had given me almost a decade before, it dawned on me. A guy like me, who had spent 3 years of college so engrossed in coming up with a viral app that no investment bank or graduate school would take him because his transcript was full of Cs, could still make billions by founding a religion. If Jesus Christ (whose last name starts with a C, so how bad could that letter really be on a transcript?) had risen from the dead today, not only would he have been the spiritual epicenter of the world (and have been the subject of so many *BuzzFeed* articles for all of the miracles he performed), but he would also have been richer than the 100 richest people in the world combined. Same would have been true of the founder of every other major religion.

And with that sudden realization, I spent the next 8 years of my life pulling a Bruce Wayne. The only differences were that my parents had not been killed in a back alleyway, I was not travelling the world to learn all of the fighting and detective skills that I would need to beat organized crime, and I was not going to dress up in a bat costume to achieve my goals. Instead, I studied the teachings of every major religion and tapped into the psychology of it all, going to various worship events to try to figure out why people were so caught up in their respective religion. It took a long time, but as I studied and studied, I was able to combine the strongest aspects of every major religion and throw in a few things that would broaden my appeal to those not so interested in religion—such as telling all those people driven by wealth, like me, that wealth was not necessarily a bad thing and would not cost them their spot in eternal paradise. All they had to do was provide a small amount to various charitable organizations and, of course, provide a small percentage to the church (i.e., me). I was convinced that I had something whose debut would be as celebrated as that of the iPhone.

In order to get the word out quickly, I decided to go the online video route, which meant that YouTube was the best way to go. And like Psy's video for *Gangam Style*, my videos presenting the Church of the Rain Droplet went viral, snagging millions of views a day. Yes, the first few videos were circulated less to spread the religion and more as a "Look at how crazy this guy is! You have to watch this video!"—but ultimately, this worked in my favor. Not only did the hundreds of millions of hits guarantee me a steady stream of revenue, but it also meant that as people started paying attention to what I was saying, my church took off. Everything that Mr. Phen had told me about founding a religion was true. Why design an app that would stop paying $50,000/day once everyone had downloaded it, when you could create a religion that told its followers to send money to their spiritual leader for as long as they lived?

So after two years of making viral videos and preaching to the many who surfed the internet in need of a spiritual center, the Church of the Rain Droplet reached $1 billion in assets. And, because transparency was a tenant of the church, my own net worth hit $100 million, which, while not Bill Gates money, would eventually reach Bill Gates money if invested wisely. The happiness I felt may not have won me my place in the afterlife of one of the other major religions, but I was doing just fine in my current one, and that was fine by me.

At first, I hid my involvement with the Church of the Rain Droplet from my parents, lest they freak out the way that David Sedaris's parents must have after he published *Me Talk Pretty One Day*. Unfortunately, it was only a matter of time before they discovered that I was the one behind what *The New York Times* had called "The fastest growing religion of all-time." When my parents finally confronted me, it was difficult for me to "respectfully" disagree with them, until at one point, having had enough, I simply explained to them that in a little less than 3 years, the Church of the Rain Droplet had amassed $1 billion in assets, which meant that those "silly YouTube videos" were not so silly anymore. When my mother heard the numbers, she was shocked, though not in the crazy mother way that she had when she first stumbled upon me in a bloody mess with a pile of baby teeth. On the other hand, my father, strangely enough, visibly swelled with pride at seeing those numbers. After one of those awkward hugs that included a double pat on the back, my father handed me a small felt pouch. Inside, much to my surprise, were my baby teeth, preserved in bronze.

"What took you so long? I thought you were going to hit that number years ago," he said with a smile. "I just hope that with all of your money you can buy your way into heaven."

"Dad, the Church of the Rain Droplet doesn't concern itself with those kinds of things. Besides, as its spiritual head, my place is already assured."

My father laughed and asked me how one went about becoming one of the church's followers. I put my arm around him and smiled, excited to have added him to my flock.

Make a Wish

A day did not pass that Marta did not kick herself for stupidly wasting her three wishes.

Yes, there were times, sitting in one of her numerous mansions in the heart of the Hollywood Hills, that she could wrap herself up with the knowledge that she was indeed (i) the wealthiest person in the world; (ii) the most beautiful person in the world; and (iii) immortal, meaning that she had forever to enjoy her unparalleled wealth and beauty. Unfortunately, while wonderful, what were beauty, wealth, and eternal life without all of the other things, or people, necessary to make those things worthwhile? All of Marta's friends had grown old and died, and all the money and beauty in the world was meaningless if she could never find that special someone to enjoy it with. If anything, her three wishes had opened up a Pandora's Box of necessary subsequent wishes that led to even more necessary wishes so that suddenly, what started off as three wishes, really required thousands upon thousands of wishes. Marta had once spent two months creating a diagram of all of the wishes that she would have had to make to justify her initial choices. The chart had resembled an evolutionary diagram of the Animal Kingdom.

If she had been really smart, she would have made a single wish, the only one that truly mattered: "I wish that everything I wish for comes true." Then she would not have had to worry about friends dying or never finding her soulmate—all she would have had to do was wish something and it would have come true. A close second would have been to wish to free the genie that had granted her the wishes in the first place. Then, with any luck, she would have a lifelong friend, like Aladdin's genie, who would grant her unlimited wishes out of a sense of friendship rather than obligation.

But no, she had stupidly wasted her three wishes in less than 2 minutes, the same amount of time it took for her to choose between an Americano or a latte at Starbucks. Even the genie was unable to mask his look of surprise at how quickly she decided on her wishes. If only there were a way she could go back in time and stop herself.

But alas, there was nothing she could do. So, instead of enjoying all of the wonderful things in her life that beauty, wealth, and eternal life provided, all she could do was think about how stupid she had been and that maybe, just maybe, she would have been happier if she had never purchased that stupid lamp in the first place.

Wax On, Wax Off

When asked why he had picked a fight with the school bully—
a mountain of a boy who had more than 50 pounds on the
next largest student at Kingsley Elementary—Jefferson
explained that he had wanted to know whether Mr. Miyagi's
training techniques actually worked. Speaking from his
hospital bed while recovering from surgery to repair a
fractured skull and shattered forearm, Jefferson sounded
relatively upbeat about the incident.

"Look, everyone at school knows how much of a jerk
Peter can be. It's about time that someone finally stood up to
him. I was amazed that all of that 'Wax on, Wax Off' stuff
actually worked. The only problem was that, because I spent
so much time working on my defense, I had no way of fighting
back. I'm going to spend more time on the 'Drum Technique'
from the second movie so that I can dish out some damage
instead of just narrowly avoiding being a punching bag."

When pressed about why he had chosen to follow
training techniques from a movie instead of going to a
traditional karate or self-defense class, Jefferson smiled and
said that it was simply more efficient.

"I love the *Karate Kid* movies, and by following the
training techniques of Mr. Miyagi, I not only got to watch the

movies over and over again in order to make sure I was doing everything correctly, but I got to actually live as if I were Daniel Larusso. Every time I waxed my dad's car or painted the garage a different color, I was actually living the movie. And of course, my parents were happy that they got to drive around in a car that always looked brand new."

Jefferson plans to continue with the training and hopes that the next time, he won't be the one to end up in the hospital.

"I mean, my second favorite movie series is *Rocky*. *Rocky* didn't win until his second attempt. Maybe I'll win the second time around, too."

Seven Important Things Jasper Kang Did Before the End of the World

At some point between the ages of 8 and 9, Jasper Kang learned the exact date and time that the world would end. Unfortunately, that fateful day was not in some remote and distant future, hundreds of years after Jasper would have passed away. Jasper could not treat it the way he did all of the dates his teachers made him memorize for his weekly quizzes—dutifully scribbled down for a grade and then filed away in his memory until it was needed for his future appearance on *Jeopardy!*. Instead, the end of the world fell squarely on Jasper's 37th birthday at 12:26 p.m. EST. And while 37 seemed a long ways away, it still loomed large in Jasper's mind. The 8-year-old was scared shitless of the day that he would turn 37.

At first, Jasper's parents chalked it up to an overactive imagination. However, after being called to the principal's office to discuss their son's presentation on "What I Want to Be When I Grow Up" titled "It Does Not Matter What You Are When You Grow Up Because Everyone is Going to Die," they begged their only son not to talk about the end of the world anymore.

"Jasper, you have to promise us that you will stop with all of the end of the world stuff. You can say those things to us, but people out there won't understand. Promise us you will."

While Jasper promised his parents that he would indeed stop, he knew that he would spend the eternity of his afterlife full of regret if he did not warn those he cared about of their impending doom. Much of elementary and middle school was spent sharing his golden nugget the way that Spider-Man and Superman shared their secret identities—only with those he could completely trust (and would not report him to their teacher for spreading paranoid delusions). During middle school, his close group of friends nodded along with his doom and gloom rants and appeared to believe his warnings. But high school was a completely different story. If Jasper had known that moving cities was going to cause such upheaval in his life, he would have begged his parents not to leave.

High school for Jasper was the darkest time in his life. Having spent the previous years of his life scheming about how to maximize his limited time on earth, he had not actually *done* anything. He had not played sports or developed any talents. His classmates viewed him as one of the "Sci-Fi" kids, like the ones who played *Magic: The Gathering* and *Dungeons & Dragons*. But Jasper envied those kids—at least they had each other. Jasper spent high school as an outcast, always on the outside looking in.

As time passed, the weight of his knowledge wore on him, causing a deep loneliness that made him consider ending his life. While other high school seniors were obsessed with how to "change the world" or "fight global warning," Jasper was busy just being sad. No one wanted the sad-looking transfer student sitting with them at lunch time.

Things would have gotten really bad for Jasper had he not had an epiphany on his first night of college. Jasper's RA made all 32 of the first years living on the 11th floor of John Jay gather in the tiny common room meant to house only half their number in order to play the standard ice breaker games intended to artificially foster camaraderie and community. And while Jasper hated icebreakers as much as the rest of the 17 and 18-year-olds squeezed in the cramped common room, one of the games caught Jasper's attention. He watched intently as his RA handed out a roll of toilet paper and instructed people to take as many or as few pieces as they wanted. Jasper had seen this done before and knew that each person would be asked to share something about himself or herself for each piece of toilet paper taken (inwardly, he laughed with maniacal glee at the football player already wearing his jersey who had taken at least 40 pieces); however, the RA surprised him by asking each person to share a goal that they wanted to accomplish instead of a fact about themselves. Jasper, along with at least a dozen others, looked straight at the football star in training and wondered how many of his "goals" would involve touchdowns. Jasper had taken only one piece of toilet paper and thought it would be easy to come up with a goal, but his mind drew a complete blank. By the time it was his turn, he copped out and joked that he hoped "to graduate in four years." He felt a deep sense of shame that his only real goal, despite knowing of the exact date of the end of the world for a decade, was to prepare for it. But Jasper was surprised to find that listening to his floormates gave him hope, and ultimately, an idea. Inspired by Nick Hornby, one of the world's best listmakers, Jasper vowed to come up with a list of 1,001 things to do before he died. If he managed to accomplish at least 80% of them, assuming that the 1,001 things were all worth doing, he would be able to say that he had lived a life worth living. All before the age of 37.

During that first semester, while most freshmen struggled with all of the things that college freshman typically struggle with, Jasper spent his time coming up with his list. The first 100 were easy enough—things like graduate from college, pay back student loans, and fall in love. But as the list grew, Jasper spent more and more time staring at the blinking cursor on his computer screen than actually coming up with things that he wanted to do before the end of the world. By the time he got to the 300s, he found that 9 out of every 10 things that he wanted to do involved either something to eat or a place to visit. Though it took him three and a half weeks to finish, and cost him a place on the Dean's List for the semester (Number 634), Jasper finally finished his list of 1,001 Important Things to Do Before the End of the World (finishing the list was Number 967).

And so, from the age of 18 through 37, Jasper diligently worked through his list, which included, among other things, the following:

37. <u>Publish a Book</u>. While Jasper considered winning the Nobel Prize in Literature (Number 3) to be one of the 20% of things he knew that he would never be able to cross off his

list, he reasoned that publishing a book was absolutely possible. When publishers and agents did not bother responding to his queries, he did what any other person who needed to cross "Publish a Book" off their to-do list would do: he self-published an e-book. Though this strategy made it harder for him to cross off "Have a Book Tour" (Number 38), he managed to arrange for three separate readings, which, surprisingly enough, were attended by a total of 14 people, only 12 of whom were his friends. And, as an added bonus, the small "book tour" helped him cross off a number of other things on his list, including "Go on a Road Trip" (Number 387), "Visit the Grand Canyon" (Number 544), and "Re-enact the Last Scene of *The Shawshank Redemption*" (Number 634), which he did before "Surfing at Santa Monica Beach" (Number 899).

212. <u>Watch a Sunrise on Victoria Peak</u>. Hong Kong had fascinated Jasper since he watched his first Jackie Chan movie (meeting Jackie Chan was Number 911, which he half checked off when he saw him from a distance at La Guardia Airport). A trip to Hong Kong would satisfy twelve things on the list, the most important of which he had been told by his friend Bill, an exchange student from the University of Hong Kong who had been completely fascinated by his roommate's vivid though morbid imagination, was to watch a sunrise on Hong Kong's highest point. So, a few hours before he was set to leave for Tokyo (Number 213), Jasper threw on a pair of shorts and a t-shirt and began a slow jog up Victoria Peak (because, as Bill told him, "There's no better way to enjoy that perfect sunrise than after running up that big hill. It'll feel like you scaled Mount Everest (Number 157, something Jasper

knew he would never do but was worth having on the list just in case)). What Bill had not told him was that the reason why everything was so wonderful when you reached the top, which it was—that sunrise was the most beautiful Jasper had ever seen—was because of how terrible the smog was on the way up there. Dripping gallons of sweat and wheezing from the smog, the beauty of the sunrise may have been amplified by the relief Jasper felt at no longer having to expend energy running up that hill. As he watched the sunrise, he vowed never to run in conditions such as those again, lest he do so much damage to his lungs that he never made it to his 37th birthday.

221. <u>Complete a Half Marathon</u>. Number 220 had originally been "Train for a Half Marathon" until his sometimes acquaintance Cassidy Pringle said that she just "didn't get" all of those people who had to train for half marathons ("It's all those same fat people that make going to yoga so unbearable" she would say). It would have been a full marathon had it not been for his doctor's warnings that his knees would not be able to handle it following reconstructive knee surgery to repair injuries from a freak accident playing intramural basketball (in fact, his doctor would have forbidden him from participating in a half marathon, but Jasper did not think that successfully running a 10K had the same ring as successfully running a half marathon). Of all the half marathons, Jasper ultimately chose to run the Brooklyn Half because he had heard that, other than a very small hill in Prospect Park, the course was basically downhill. It was the perfect half marathon for a guy who was not supposed to run one. What no one told him was that the subway trip back was

going to be an absolute nightmare, with each runner and their corresponding cheering section doing their best to push their way onto overpacked trains to get back to the city from Coney Island. New Yorkers did not need people paid to pack them into subways the way the Japanese did. If someone wanted to get onto a train, they were going to do it.

392. <u>Win the Lottery</u>. After spending over $350 on Mega Millions tickets, Jasper finally accepted that 1 out of 250 million were terrible odds and that the end of the world would come and go without him winning $100,000,000.00 (Number 422). Instead, he turned to scratch-and-win tickets. Jasper scratched and scratched until he finally won $5. It was not life-changing, but it was enough to buy another ticket (which, unsurprisingly, did not win him any money).

544. <u>Bet It All on Black</u>. Jasper wondered whether Rudyard Kipling really believed that you were only a man if you could pick yourself up after betting and losing everything. When Jasper had added this item to the list, he did not have a clear understanding of what "betting it all" actually meant, but he forged ahead anyway and emptied out his savings account before hopping onto a bus at Port Authority and heading to Atlantic City. Unfortunately, when he exchanged his $2500 for a measly few chips, he chickened out. He went on to bet $100, won when the small white ball finally settled on 29 black, cashed his chips, and caught the next bus back to the City. He may not have been a man according to Rudyard Kipling, but riding back on the bus $100 richer, he felt man enough to himself.

892. <u>Toss a Penny into Niagara Falls</u>. If Jasper had known that tossing a penny into the Falls could have gotten him fined or arrested for littering, he would never have done it (or put it on the list; he had in fact added toss a penny off the Empire State Building, but scratched it off when he realized that he could have been convicted for second-degree murder if the penny landed on an unsuspecting passerby). But he did throw a penny into the torrential Niagara River, vowing not to share the wish accompanying that penny into the rapid waters in the hopes that he would be able to somehow avoid the inevitable.

1,000. <u>Smoke a Cigar the Night Before the End of the World</u>. While others in high school and college had experimented heavily with smoking anything that could be smoked, Jasper had stood to the side and watched, wondering whether any would ever invite him to take part. When no invitation came, instead of simply going out and buying his own smokes, Jasper simply never smoked anything. By the time he reached his thirties, he felt like he may as well wait until he reached 36 years and 364 days old before smoking for the first time (and he felt that the run up Victoria Peak, as well as his visits to Shanghai (Number 112) and Beijing (Number 113) with all of the smog had already done enough damage to his lungs). And so, for the occasion, Jasper took a single Montecristo No. 2, a cigar he had been assured was top-notch, and smoked it from the rooftop of his small one-bedroom apartment, hoping that he would somehow live to see his 38th birthday (Number 1,001).

Unfortunately, Jasper never crossed that last one off his list.

Encyclopedia of the New York We Used to Know

Borders

The first time that you laid eyes on her was at the Borders on Broadway just west of Wall Street. She was lying on her stomach on the carpeted floor wearing a bright yellow dress with a stack of magazines to her right, her legs kicked up behind her as if she were reenacting the first time that Humbert Humbert laid eyes on Lolita (or at least reenacting how you thought that initial encounter went, as you had never read the book and could only vaguely recall scenes from the trailer for one of the movie adaptations, most likely the Jeremy Irons version, but you were not sure). That image alone would have been enough to capture your attention, but the fact that she was surrounded by men in gray and navy suits on their lunch break who appeared as equally enamoured by her as you (who happened to be dressed in a navy suit) while sneaking a peek over whatever magazines they were reading, made her all the more alluring.

You picked up a magazine at random off of the nearest rack—an issue of *GQ*, how lucky for you, you thought to yourself—and stood a few feet to her right, just out of her field of view, or so you thought. As you alternated leafing through the magazine and watching her flip through a copy of *Cosmo*, you wondered what it would take for you to summon up the courage to start up a conversation with her. Countless people had done it before, made that initial move, or so magazines like the very one you were reading would have you believe, so why not you?

"So, are you done checking out my ass, or are you going to introduce yourself?" she asked without so much as looking up from her magazine.

You dropped the issue of *GQ* to the ground before looking around to see if she was addressing any of her other admirers. Unfortunately, or fortunately, you were clearly the one who she was addressing, or at least the only one who had not immediately taken a few steps back at the sound of her voice. If only you had been a few seconds faster, you could have been one of the many just a few feet too far to be the target of her chastisement instead of the one caught directly in her sights.

But instead of allowing the nearly uncontrollable urge to run take hold, you smiled and said the first words that came to mind: "Hi, sorry about that. My name is Quentin. What's yours?"

WD-50

Even before the first course arrives, you wonder why so many guys in New York thought that taking someone to a fancy restaurant was the way to a person's heart. Did they really think that the price of an extravagant meal could compensate for whatever else they were lacking? Mind you, you were never one to turn down a free meal. In fact, you joked with your friends that no matter how unattractive you found someone, you always gave a person three chances to prove you wrong. Even if the dates and conversation were bad, you could at least try various places around the city that you may not otherwise get to enjoy (and, if you were being honest with yourself, given that the $22,000/year grant you received as part of your PhD program at Columbia University did not go very far, you had no problems enjoying those places on someone else's dime).

When you met Quentin a few days ago at Borders, doing your best to feign disgust and indignation while also trying to stifle some laughter as you watched his face go beet red after you did your best to shame him and all of the other would-be Wall Street perverts, you were shocked when you found yourself giving him your phone number. You were even more shocked when you agreed to go to dinner a few days later when he called. When he told you that he had seen you reading an article about Wylie Dufresne and that he wanted to take you to WD-50, you did your best to hide your confusion over the phone.

"Yes, I've always wanted to go there," you lied. You had no idea what on Earth he was talking about—had you really been reading an article about a chef?—and you had no idea what WD-50 was. It did not matter how famous this chef was. There was simply no way that a restaurant that sounded like it could be used to fix a squeaky door could be all that appetizing.

After hanging up the phone, you immediately scoured the internet to figure out why on Earth Wylie Dufresne was such a big deal and why Quentin seemed convinced on the phone that you would be impressed by dinner at WD-50. As you watched each of the courses being placed in front of you, you realized that, no matter how many hours you had spent trying to understand molecular gastronomy, nothing was going to prepare you for this cavalcade of food. You were barely able to identify, let alone stomach, some of the things that Quentin seemed to eat without hesitation—did he really enjoying eating the Chilled Egg Drop Soup with Sea Urchin or the Cuttlefish with Carrot and Schmaltz?

"Carol, isn't this food amazing?"

"I think so? It's just so different from anything I've ever had before," you replied.

"Sometimes different is good, right?"

"I guess," you said, doing your best not to roll your eyes at the obvious line.

Luckily for Quentin, the dessert was to die for. You had never had a hazelnut tart before, but you knew if you had your way, you would be eating as many as you could in the future.

When you snuck a peak at the bill, however, you knew that you would likely not be having any more hazelnut tarts at WD-50. Or at least, you would not be having any hazelnut tarts at WD-50 on your dime.

Filene's Basement

Carol first tells you that she loves you on your third date after the two of you had to rush through Union Square in search of a bathroom. Instead of dinner, you had both decided to have drinks that evening. While drinks were good, you quickly realized that an endless flow of overpriced cocktails was going to seriously hurt your wallet (and likely end up with one of you passed out at the bar), so you suggested dessert as a next destination. Unfortunately, one of you had not gone to the bathroom before leaving that particular establishment.

"We have to get out. I need a bathroom right now," she said.

Rather than try to make it to either of your apartments—which you thought may have made you look a little presumptuous so early in your relationship—you told her to follow you as you hopped off the train at Union Square and then proceeded to snake your way through all of the slow-moving tourists to Filene's Basement. Instead of heading to the nearest bathroom, the one she wanted to run to, you grabbed her arm and rushed to the top floor.

"Wait, isn't this for employees only?"

"You mean that sign," you said, pointing to the "Employees Only" sign above the hallway. "It's not a reference to the bathrooms. It's a reference to the employees' lounge. Everyone can use the bathroom."

"I love you. You're such a genius."

As you saw her rush into the bathroom, past a somewhat bewildered looking employee, you wondered whether she registered what she had said to you. While you were not inclined to say it back, even three dates in you were pretty certain that there would come a time when you would say it back and mean it.

Barnes & Noble

Given the circumstances of the way you met, it was not surprising that bookstores were not only a standard meeting place, but a destination in which the two of you could spend hours together. Because you were getting your PhD in environmental studies and he worked as a paralegal at one of those law firms on Wall Street that no one had ever heard of, the Barnes & Noble at 66th St. and Broadway, about halfway between the two, quickly became a place that you met and spent many an evening. While you often brought along undergraduate papers to grade and materials for your dissertation, you knew that no work was going to get done. Instead, each of you would fill a basket with books and magazines and then camp out on the third floor near the café—one of you would purchase a coffee so you could observe the "Reserved for Café Customers" signs on every table—and slowly work through your respective hauls. If someone needed to get more, that person would go off and lose themselves in the aisles while the other continued to hold down your spot.

The time spent at that Barnes & Noble would come to be some of your happiest. It was only when it was time to leave that things always took a turn for the worse. While you collected the items that you read and went about the somewhat tedious task of putting each back where you found them, exactly as your kindergarten teacher Ms. Rose had taught you, Quentin simply stacked his items up and left them on a table for an employee to put back.

"Can you please hurry up? Why do you bother returning everything? It's literally someone's job to do that."

"Really?"

"It's exactly like at a movie theater. At the end of the movie, once everyone has left, people come in to clean everything up before the next movie starts. Why take that responsibility away from them? Why make them obsolete?"

"I don't know what's worse. The fact that you're too lazy to return those books or that you have come up with a logical explanation for it."

H&H Bagels

The morning after the first night that you stayed over, you snuck out early to grab breakfast from H&H Bagels. As far as you were concerned, whether it was because of the water or because food critics had long had a New York bias, there was simply nothing better than a New York bagel. And no place made a better New York bagel than H&H Bagels.

When you got back to your apartment, excited at the chance of finally introducing Carol to one of the best things the city had to offer, you were rather disappointed to find her still fast asleep. While part of you wanted to crawl back into bed beside her, this was too important of a moment to delay. How had she lived in the city for three years and not visited the bagel mecca of the world?

After doing your best to stomp around the apartment, pretending to clean up and get your apartment in order, she finally came out of your bedroom, rubbing the sleep out of her eyes and clearly doing her best not to look too irritated at the noise.

"Sorry, did I wake you?"

"What do you think?"

"Well, sorry about that, but I have a surprise for you."

"I love surprises."

"Guess what I have for us? H&H Bagels!"

As you handed her a bagel along with a tub of cream cheese, excited for the praise and thanks that was surely going to be showered upon you the moment she took a bite—and, if you were lucky, would carry over back to the bedroom, as you had really enjoyed yourself last night—she looked up at you and then over at the kitchen.

"Do you have a toaster?"

"Why would you need a toaster?"

"I don't know, to toast my bagel?"

"Seriously?"

"Uh, yes, seriously?"

"Everyone knows that a true New York bagel doesn't need to be toasted. In fact, it shouldn't be toasted."

"You say tomat-oh, I say tom-ah-to. Who cares?"

"Well, I don't have a toaster, sorry."

"That's okay," she said as she put it back into the brown bag. "I'll just take it back to my place and warm it up there."

"Okay," you said, doing your best to hide your disappointment as you began to slice open your bagel.

Daffy's

You did not understand why Quentin seemed so averse to shopping at a discount retailer, or based on his moaning, even stepping foot in one, but there was no way that you were ever going to pay full price for designer clothing when there was simply no need to. He may have been paranoid that someone from his office was going to see him and think that he had been lying when he said that all of his suits were custom-made, but you did not share any of those fears. (You also wondered whether the lawyers at Quentin's firm laughed at him behind his back because, even to an untrained eye like your own, it was clear that Quentin bought his suits off the rack like most people did.)

While you had nothing against shopping per se—in fact, you loved shopping for comfortable clothing that you could wear around campus—you had very little to no interest in shopping for formal attire. In fact, you had no interest in it whatsoever until two days ago when Quentin asked what you would be wearing to his firm's holiday party.

"I'm just going to throw something on or borrow something from Jennifer or Angela."

Apparently, that had not been the appropriate response, and he had insisted that you go out and buy something new. When he did not so much as offer any other guidance other than "Pick out something nice. You know, something for a fancy cocktail party," you insisted that he throw on a coat because there was no way that you were going to go shopping without him.

While he had thought that you would be dragging him to Bloomingdale's or Saks Fifth Avenue, he had been shocked when you told him you would instead be going to Daffy's, and if Daffy's didn't have anything, T.J. Maxx. But once he got over his initial shock, he ended up buying much more than you. Instead of him being the one to moan and groan over how many dresses you were trying on—he only had to look at two as you found something perfect almost immediately, which was, of course, 85% off—it was you who kept looking at your watch and wondering what on Earth he was doing in the dressing room.

By the time the two of you had paid, your bill had come to $68.56 for the dress, and his had come up to $354.53 for a suit, overcoat, and three ties.

Roseland Ballroom

When you had suggested that the two of you see a concert together, you had had something different in mind than tagging along with her and some of her friends from out of town for Jimmy Eat World. Without having heard a single song, with a name like that, you were certain that you were not going to like them. Gone were the days when you actually looked forward to turning on the radio and discovering new music because all you were greeted with was either boy band ballads or pop punk noise. You wondered which of the two the band would be.

Much to your surprise, it was not terrible. The music was a little bit whiny (Carol said the term I was looking for was "emo"), but not so over the top so as to make the music bad. You managed to have a good time jumping up and down with all of the people pressed against one another on the dance floor. That is, until, you lost a flip-flop in the crowd and all you could think about was how you were a pinprick away from having some terrible disease enter your blood stream.

"Hey, are you okay?" she asked.

"Yeah. Yeah, of course, why wouldn't I be?"

The music and all of the people all around may have been happy and upbeat, but all you could think about was finding your flip-flop, something that did not happen until an hour later when the concert was over and everyone was streaming for the exits.

Avalon

You had never been one to enjoy clubbing—did people really think that it was fun to go to a place where the music was so loud you could not talk to anyone, one drink was more expensive than a bottle of wine from a liquor store, and the dance floor was really no different than rush hour on a crowded train?—but he had insisted that you had never really experienced clubbing because you had never experienced bottle service. When you asked him how he was going to afford it, he simply smiled and told you not to worry about it. What he meant, as you found out within a few minutes of him escorting you past the security guard stationed in front of some velvet ropes, was that a young associate at his law firm had found out that he passed the bar and decided to drop some money that should have been going towards his law school loans to celebrate with a bunch of people who he barely knew. Although you had to admit that there was something cool about the special service, you ultimately found the whole experience rather uninspired. The amount of money that was spent on the table was apparently "well over" $2,000, which seemed to impress Quentin, but which you thought was rather wasteful.

"Come on. Tell me you didn't have a lot of fun."

"Look, it was fun to be able to sit back there and have those drinks, but it wasn't worth $2,000."

"I totally agree, but it's not like we were spending anything."

"No, but didn't you say to him that when you pass the bar, you're going to do something like this too?"

"Yeah, but come on. I'm just applying to law school now. It's going to be like four years before I do anything like this."

"But when you graduate, you're going to have loans to pay back, aren't you?"

"I don't want to fight about this. We're fighting about something we may or may not fight about years from now. Let's just go to sleep, okay?"

Pearl River Mart

After you moved in together—which was really her deciding that it was time to kick your roommate out, tear down the temporary wall that had been put up so as to turn your one-bedroom apartment into an incredibly small, living room-less, two-bedroom apartment—you spent a lot of time together going to IKEA and Pearl River Mart to decorate the living room. Not a lot was purchased during those visits, but she insisted that you come with her, a little like when she forced you to accompany her to Daffy's so that she could buy a dress for one of your holiday parties.

"Look, right now, this is still really your apartment. And there's not much I can do with your bedroom. But the living room? That's a space that both of us can decorate together."

Who were you to argue with her? You were just happy to not have to leave work clothing at her apartment for nights when she did not want to come back to yours. So you begrudgingly agreed to trek to whatever places she wanted to go to in order to spruce up the place. And, unsurprisingly enough, she had the same approach to decorating that she had to clothes—discounted and on the cheap. Although initially you had not been on board when it had come to buying clothing, after having been introduced to the world of discount shopping, you were completely in support of scouring places for a deal. You were, of course, particularly supportive because you would rather split the cost of cheap items from Pearl River Mart than to split the cost of more expensive items from places like Crate & Barrel or ABC Carpet & Home.

Although you pretended to be annoyed at being dragged constantly to a place where most people went to buy cheap party favors, you were just happy to see how happy she was to move in with you. At first, she had seemed a little hesitant, but when you told her that you would allow her to decorate the living room, she seemed much more excited. She had been living in a three-bedroom apartment with her friends Lily and Paloma who believed that all major apartment decisions, including decorating, needed to be put to a vote. Unfortunately for Carol, Lily and Paloma were sisters who had a way of voting as a bloc whenever major decisions needed to be made. This included how to decorate the living room, which explained why instead of a couch, their living room had beanbag chairs.

So, when she finally had the chance to decorate your living room, who were you to stop her? You were just glad to finally never have to commute to see her again.

Kim's Video and Music

It may have been a product of him trying to impress people at work or a carryover from growing up in the city, but from very early on in your relationship, he seemed to always feel the need to exude how cool he was. He always talked about wanting to check out the hottest restaurants or how the next cool band would be playing at such and such a bar. None of this was a problem because he rarely forced you to go to anything—that did not stop you, of course, from accompanying him to Nobu and Grammercy Tavern—which allowed you to do what most PhD students did: work on your dissertation and read. Each of your natural tendencies provided just the amount of space that the other needed, which was especially important after you moved in together.

One area, however, that did continue to irk you was that whenever he went up to campus to meet you, he almost always insisted on meeting at Kim's. This, in and of itself, was not a problem; however, any time he wanted a few minutes inside meant a gruelling affair of listening to him go on and on about bands that only people who shopped at places like Kim's instead of HMV or Tower Records knew about (which, looking back on it, made you wonder why he agreed to go to a Jimmy Eat World concert). Whenever he put on one of the CDs that he just purchased, you always did your best to pretend that you enjoyed it, not wanting to ruin his mood.

"Don't you love this? This band is going to be huge."

"Yeah, it's really great," you replied, wondering why he could not simply put on a U2 album. There was a reason why U2 and Whitney Houston were so popular and sold so many albums and most indie artists did not—they were actually good.

Pearl Paint

Every time she returns from Pearl Paint with bags of paint supplies and blank canvases, you do your best not to make a big deal out of it. You would have been completely supportive of her if it did not seem as if she were more interested in shopping for paint supplies rather than actually painting. She had not only filled the closet beside the doorway full of her supplies, but she had also started filling up the living room with a number of blank canvases of varying shapes and sizes and dozens of unopened paint bottles. How many bottles of black paint did she really need? How many bottles did anyone need?

"Why do you insist on buying all of these paint supplies if you never use them?"

"I do use them! What do you call those canvases in our closet that you won't let me hang?"

"I've never stopped you from hanging them. Every time I ask when you're going to finish one, you tell me soon and that when you do finish, you're going to start putting them up."

"Yeah, because there is *so* much space on the walls, maybe they will fit in a sliver of space between some of the lame Salvador Dalí posters you seem to think make you artsy."

Crumbs

Most people who had to name a favorite cupcake in the city usually said Magnolia's, but there was really only one cupcake place for you: Crumbs. Unlike those who talked about how cupcakes needed to be light and fluffy and have just the right amount of frosting, which is likely why Magnolia's did so well, you were really all about size, which absolutely shocked Quentin when you explained why you were touched, but not floored, by the box of Magnolia's cupcakes that he had bought for your birthday (you did, however, make sure to quickly explain yourself as you did not want a repeat of the H&H Bagels incident, which resulted in him sulking for a week). No, if you had to choose a cupcake, it was Crumbs all the way. Although he, along with the rest of your friends, were always taken aback by your insistence that it was the best cupcake around, they certainly all agreed that you *believed* what you were saying when they saw you attack a giant peanut butter cup or red velvet cupcake. You may have eaten healthily generally, often packing salads and sandwiches to enjoy between teaching classes or office hours, but when you wanted dessert, you did not want to eat small pieces of cake or teeny tiny bites of something sweet—you wanted to eat something massive. Crumbs never let you down.

After he had seen firsthand how disappointed you were with the Magnolia cupcakes—though you would likely not have been disappointed if you had been allowed to eat two or three of them, but he had bought the box of twelve to share with him and your friends—and then how happy eating a giant Crumbs cupcake made you, he quickly became a Crumbs fan too. Even if he did not think that the cupcakes were that good, he seemed to like how happy they made you (and provided him with a place to go whenever you were upset with him), which was more than enough reason for him to turn Crumbs into his go-to place as well.

Ziegfeld Theatre

You were absolutely shocked when one of the partners called you into his office that morning to say that he wanted to give you two tickets to the premier of *Gangs of New York* that he was no longer able to use. Apparently, he had heard how hard you had been working and thought that the associates were rewarded enough and that maybe a paralegal ought to be rewarded. To say that you were excited was an understatement.

Unfortunately, Carol did not seem to share your excitement. She seemed to have little interest in getting dressed up for a movie, even if it meant the chance to rub elbows with Leonardo Dicaprio, Cameron Diaz, and Daniel Day-Lewis.

But after watching her reluctantly put on the same dress that she had worn to your firm's last three holiday parties, you wondered whether you should have gone with someone else.

Luckily, you had not found a stand-in. Not only had she walked out of the theatre gushing at how amazing the movie was, she also could not stop talking about how nice Leo had been. He had not only stopped to take a few pictures with her, but he even chatted for a few minutes about his work regarding climate change.

That night, you went to bed pleased that you had insisted that she attended.

FAO Schwarz

There was no way for you to know that he was going to propose that evening. In fact, given that the two of you had been fighting quite a bit, it seemed like taking a long break was much more likely than him getting on one knee.

The day had started out somewhat unremarkably, when you woke up to the sound of him stomping around in the kitchen. When you walked out in order to chastise him, you were pleasantly greeted with bagels and cream cheese, which he had already gone ahead and sliced and toasted for you (in the toaster that you had insisted the two of you needed for your weekend morning bagel brunches). You should have realized that something may have been up when he told you that he had made reservations that night at Marea, but you had thought that he had done so because he wanted to celebrate getting into law school. Little did you know.

On the walk over to the restaurant, you saw some tourists running into FAO Schwarz and realized that you needed to pick up a gift for your new niece.

"Can't we go after? I don't want to be late for dinner. The reservation is for 7 p.m."

"It'll only take 10 minutes. We're only a few blocks away."

He reluctantly followed you inside, which in and of itself should have told you that something was completely off. He was the one that was normally pulling you into FAO Schwarz or any other toy store when you were moving about the city because he loved buying gifts for his nephews (or at least that was the excuse he used for why he kept buying action figures, when only one out of every five ever actually left the apartment). He looked so out of it that even when you told him to head to the action figures section and that you would meet him there, he simply shook his head and said that he would follow you around. It was at that moment that you registered that something was wrong, feeling the need to hug him close and ask if anything was going on.

"Are you okay?"

"Of course I am."

"Are you sure?"

"Yes."

"Hey, what is this lumpy thing in your jacket?"

"That? Oh, it's my wallet."

"No, your wallet is down here," you laugh, cupping the back of his jeans with your right hand.

"It's nothing."

"Come on. Tell me. What's your problem?"

"Well, if this is where it has to be, then this is where it has to be. How Jerry Maguire of me."

"Oh my God."

Sports Authority

You were not sure why you kept going to Sports Authority, but you kept doing it anyway. Sometimes you dragged her along with you, other times you did not. All you knew was that if you kept buying running gear, maybe you would run more (a similar argument about her Pearl Paint spending habits had only resulted in her storming out of the apartment and returning with even more paint supplies).

It was a few weeks after proposing, after getting bombarded with questions about when the wedding was actually going to be, that you decided that you needed to find something to distract you. That something needed to also take you out of the apartment because she too was bombarding you with wedding talk.

So when someone at work who blew out his knee asked if you were interested in taking his bib for the New York City Marathon, you jumped all over it. While you had not run more than 3 miles since you started working, you used to run a fair amount in college. Once, you had even ran 10 miles for a bet to see which of your group of 5 would be forced to room together during senior year in the four-room suite that you had won in the housing lottery. Luckily, you had come in third and therefore were not stuck with sharing a room, something that would have been a disaster as you had been able to hear your friend Stanley snoring even through the wall.

When you began to run, she was pleased, most likely because you had gained a fair amount of weight since you started seeing each other (though you blamed it on work rather than being in a comfortable relationship). But after awhile, she became annoyed that you would run for so long, especially during times that most couples would spend time together, Friday nights or Sunday brunch hours. For a time, it seemed like you only fit her into your free time when you slept or when you went to Sports Authority in order to buy even more running gear to fuel your obsession.

The period of time leading up to the New York Marathon was not one of the better ones in your relationship.

5 Pointz

When you took him to see the murals and pieces at the mecca for graffiti in Long Island City, you thought that it would be something that he would enjoy. He had often commented on "cool" graffiti that you came across when moving through the City, so you thought 5 Pointz would be perfect. Unfortunately, you had not realized that the marathon was going to take so much out of him and that walking, however mild the weather was in November, was not something to suggest the day after he ran 26.2 miles. Watching him limp up and down the stairs in the subway was not how you thought that you would be spending a Monday off from work. But despite the pain, mostly his, you were certain that his mood would change the moment that he saw how cool the art was.

You were wrong.

Although he was very impressed by the art, he was of the opinion that it was only a matter of time before a developer came in and turned the space into condos or something more "useful."

"I don't see why you're so upset. Yes, the art is wonderful, but is it that different from any of the stuff we see in the Village or the Lower East Side? There will always be great murals over the City. I don't see why this one is really all that different."

"It is different. This place should be thought of as a historical monument and protected."

It was only later that evening after the fighting continued back at your apartment that you found out that one of the reasons why he was so adamant that the place be developed was that his law firm was representing developers who had long been trying to put up condos. You had always known that he worked for "The Man," but it was the first time you actually resented him for it.

Steve & Barry's

After you started receiving acceptance letters from law schools, you spent a lot of time debating which one you were going to. You were leaning towards staying in the City—NYU or Fordham—but she wanted you to go to Boston College or Boston University so that she could accept a post-doc offer at Harvard (she had done her best to hide her disappointment when you had received the rejection letter from the Big H, but did she really think you actually had a shot to get in there?). Although you were considering the Boston-area schools, it was hard for you to give up the City and besides, she had received post-doc offers at Columbia and NYU as well. If you both went to NYU, then you could study together in the library and commute home together. It seemed like the kind of story that you would want to tell people at your wedding (though you never brought that up in your arguments about where the two of you should end up, as the last thing that you wanted to do was enter into a long conversation about the wedding, the date of which had still yet to be determined even a year after the engagement).

One Sunday after watching the Knicks lose yet another dismal game, as you were making your way to K-Town for some dinner, you both stopped at the Steve & Barry's in the Manhattan Mall. You had wanted to go inside because you wanted to pick up a pair of Starbury's for the insanely "expensive" price of $14.98, while she wanted to see just how far Sarah Jessica Parker must have fallen to have to create a line to be sold exclusively at a discount retailer.

After you had finished paying—you had loaded up on three pairs of Starbury's, two to actually use and one to keep in the off-chance that they may be worth something someday—you seemed unable to find Carol, no matter how hard you looked. She was not in Sarah Jessica Parker's "Bitten" section, nor was she in the changing room. It was not until you wandered almost from one end of the store to the other that you finally stumbled upon her in the college apparel section. She was in front of a mirror, wearing a Harvard T-shirt, while holding up an NYU one.

When she looked up and saw you, she dropped the NYU T-shirt to the floor, as if she were embarrassed by what she was holding. That night, you realized that she was probably less embarrassed by being seen holding up an NYU T-shirt, than having been seen wearing a Harvard one.

Union Square Café

After the initial blitz of attending fancy restaurants and cocktail bars that filled the first six months of your relationship—you still did not understand how on Earth he managed to afford to take you to all those places on his paralegal salary—the two of you had fallen into a much more sensible routine of eating out once or twice a week at much more affordable restaurants and eating at home the remainder of the time.

But after you had decided that you were going to accept the post-doc position at Harvard and he had decided on NYU for law school, things had taken a turn for the worse. Neither of you said it, but both of you resented the other for putting their career ahead of the relationship. Both of you said that Boston to New York was not too far away and that you could simply get used to taking a bus, but the truth was that neither of you was all that sure that you could handle the distance.

In an attempt to celebrate the next stages for each of you, you had decided that splurging on a great Danny Meyer meal would hopefully help the both of you look at the good aspects your relationship and remind you of why you had gotten engaged in the first place.

Unfortunately, as wonderful as the meal was, there was nothing that seemed to be able to cut through the awkward silences and your attempts to put on a brave face. You had no problems doing long-distance, having done it once before with a boyfriend between New York and D.C. It was Quentin who kept saying things like he was not sure how often he would be able to take the bus up because he had heard that first year of law school was the hardest, and what are we going to do about our apartment, and could you help with the rent?

When the check came and it was higher than even you had expected it to be—the meal would have been much cheaper if the two of you had opted for a bottle of wine instead of the many glasses that you each ordered—you could not help but feel a little bit resentful that the meal had not been more enjoyable and that your company did not seem more satisfied.

Fung Wah Bus

As you waited with her for the bus to arrive, you wondered whether you should have indeed faked a work emergency and left. The two of you knew that things were over, that when she had returned the ring to you a week ago after dinner at Union Square Café that she really did think that there was no going back. She had said that it was merely bad timing, that if you had proposed to her a few years from now, when she was back in the City, that things would be better. But you did not think so. As far as you were concerned, the moment that she got on the bus, that would be it. You would not have been surprised if in a week or so, instead of coming back down to fill-up a U-Haul to drive her things to Cambridge, she had instead sent her brother to pick up all her things and that you would never see her again.

When the bus finally arrived and people started to board, neither of you had all that much to say to one another. Other than a wave and an awkward hug, there was no other communication between the two of you. She seemed excited to start something new and you could not imagine ever wanting to leave New York. Maybe the two of you had been a bad match from the start, but you liked to think that maybe, just maybe, the two of you would get back together a year or two from now. Your only hope was that however the two of you changed, it would be for the better, the same that way you hoped that the forever changing City would always be changing for the better, even when you were not so sure.

You could only hope.

An Oral History of Dream

At 12:32 p.m. on April 6th, 20XX, President Sarah Johnson concluded her remarks and was immediately escorted out of the White House Press Briefing Room before anyone had a chance to respond or ask any questions. President Johnson and her team need not have worried—even if anyone in the White House press corps had any questions, they would have been too shocked by her proposed remarks to respond. Those not staring straight ahead, still processing President Johnson's announcement, were busy calling and texting their loved ones in case they had missed the broadcast. While other drugs such as crack, cocaine, opiates, and the like had affected large segments of the population, Dream had affected nearly everyone. With an estimated 44% of Americans using the drug at least once a day (a statistic that many experts believed significantly underestimated the prevalence of the drug), nearly everyone was related to or knew someone under the drug's influence.

So when President Johnson made the announcement that she was invoking martial law and directing all military and local law enforcement to place anyone testing positive for Dream into one of 300 detention centers across the country, nearly everyone in the room feared that law enforcement was waiting outside the Press Briefing Room to escort any offenders to a detention center or that one of their loved ones was already being hauled away. Regardless of whether they agreed with President Johnson—and, in time, nearly everyone would—everyone knew that things would never be the same.

The end of the Dream epidemic was finally at hand.

Dr. Wilson Sanchez, Chief of Research and Development at the Starlight Institute and Joseph Baxter Professor of Physics, Cornell University

We stumbled upon the drug quite by accident. While by no means the focus of research conducted in my lab (most of our resources were directed towards studying the speed of light), we had been developing a sleeping agent that would allow people to control how many hours they slept. With so many people in the United States suffering from chronic sleep disorders—well over 75 million people, last I checked—I did not know why more resources were not being directed towards alleviating something affecting so many.

Our idea was simple: develop a sleeping agent that allowed someone to sleep exactly 8 hours, or whatever period of time he or she wanted. If we were successful, we would make the alarm clock as obsolete as a cassette player.

Megan Winters, PhD candidate

Dr. Sanchez told people that he was developing the drug in order to help those suffering from various sleep disorders, but anyone who spent more than a few seconds with him knew the truth: Dr. Sanchez was only interested in two things: money and fame.

Dr. Sanchez

Results from early trials of the drug were better than we could have hoped. Once we managed to approximate the correct dosages, which was a significantly more difficult task than I had initially thought it would be, test subjects woke up within 10 minutes of their desired time. When we were able to improve results with a second and third set of test subjects, with subjects waking up within three minutes of their desired wake-up time, we knew that we had something special.

Miles Lattimore, Test Subject from Trial Group 3

Initially, I was extremely skeptical about participating in the trial. People died from complications with anesthesia all the time and as far as I was concerned, a sleeping drug was really no different.

But, let's be honest—$500 to sleep for five nights? They wanted to pay me money to S-L-E-E-P. People talk about free money, but this was it. How could I say no? Besides, it was being sponsored by Cornell University, and they wouldn't let anything happen to us, right?

Lindsey Lam, Research Assistant to Dr. Wilson Sanchez

I worried that we were moving too quickly by having human trials before we were sure that the drug was safe; however, Dr. Sanchez did not share any of these fears. What I did not tell him, nor did I share with anyone else in the lab, was that I knew that he had forged the approvals from the Institutional Review Board and the FDA.

Miles Lattimore

I remember the first time that I kissed a girl, the first time that I slept with a girl, and the first time that I smoked a joint. As great as those moments were, they were nothing compared to the first time I tried tri-hydro-fluoro-benzyl-carbonate or whatever the hell it was. I knew that it didn't matter whether the FDA had approved the drug or not; I would do everything I could to get my hands on as much of it as possible. I mean, I don't think these people really understood what they had because none of them had ever tried it. Yes, it allowed people to wake up at 8 a.m. if that's what they wanted, but the real genius of it all was that it let you relive whatever memories you wanted. Every time I went to sleep, I got to relive that first kiss, the first time I had sex, the first time I got high. And when I woke up? I remembered everything that happened while I was asleep. What could be better than being able to actually experience, within your dreams, all of those moments in your life of pure joy? Not even the high of the best drugs out there could beat that.

Dream was better than a dream come true.

Megan Winters

Even before joining his lab, I had already heard that Dr. Sanchez was something of an egomaniac. Yes, the *idea* for Dream was his, but what did he actually know about drug and pharmaceutical development? He was a physicist for Christ's sake. And not even the useful kind, because who really cared about the practicable applications that could be gleaned from studying the speed of light? No one, that's who. Lindsey and I were the ones who actually developed the drug. The least that he could have done was give us some credit by putting our names on the research papers.

Lindsay Lam

Dr. Sanchez was a visionary. And I don't use that term loosely. He was just as demanding as Steve Jobs, directing each of us the way that I imagined that Jobs directed Apple's pioneers. While controversial, I think that he was just as successful as Jobs.

I was absolutely delighted to be a part of his work.

Megan Winters

Whenever Dr. Sanchez referred to himself as the Hispanic Steve Jobs, I had to resist the urge to either gag or laugh hysterically. When he showed up to work once in a black turtleneck and New Balance sneakers, I pretended to be sick and spent the rest of the day at home watching Netflix.

And the only reason why Lindsay didn't share my opinion of him was that she was sleeping with him.

Dr. Sanchez

I often wonder whether things would have been different if I had been more hands-on, more directly involved with the day-to-day running of the lab. Maybe I put too much trust in those in the weeds, trust that those people had not earned. Maybe then I would have noticed when samples started to go missing.

Megan Winters

Although not being named in the initial articles published in *Nature* was tough to swallow, it wasn't until Dr. Sanchez made a presentation to Cornell's Board of Trustees claiming to have "stumbled" upon the correct formulation of Dream while burning the midnight oil at the office that I decided that enough was enough. I can't remember a time that he was ever in the lab past 3 p.m. Given the amount of bullshit that he was spouting, I knew that if I was not going to ever get credit for my work, I was at least going to get rich.

Miles Lattimore

When Megan first approached me, I wanted to ask her if she was wearing a wire. I mean, what was I supposed to think? She said the two of us could get rich. All we had to do was steal as much of it from her lab as we could, find a way to distribute it in New York and other major cities, and not get caught. What could go wrong?

Megan Winters

I'm not proud to admit it, but I chose to approach Miles because of the track marks that I had seen along his arms. He had disclosed a prior history of drug use when he filled out the initial participant form, something that would normally have disqualified him from participating in a study; however, Dr.

Sanchez wanted participants of all backgrounds and medical histories, including people with prior, or what I suspected in Miles's case, current, drug history. Despite the risks, who was I to argue with the Hispanic Steve Jobs?

Tony Williams, Mayor of New York

New York has weathered a number of drug crises—heroin, crack, opioids—but nothing compared to Dream. I believe that it was so different due to its very nature. People weren't doing this drug at clubs or outside on a stoop or even with their friends. They were doing it in the privacy of their homes, in the comfort of their beds. You didn't even suspect that someone was on the drug until he or she called in sick every day for two weeks.

Lindsey Lam

While I realized early on that the drug had psychotropic properties, it was hard to determine what those properties were. Participants kept waking up and begging for another dose, their explanations usually incoherent, like insisting that they needed to speak to their dead father or profess their love to their soul mate. I feared that the drug had hallucinatory effects, but Dr. Sanchez dismissed my concerns, noting that after a few minutes of waking up, participants returned to their normal state. I knew that the only way I would know for certain what was happening would be to try it myself. I was a researcher and that's what researchers do. When I woke up six hours and one minute after going to bed, having spent the night reliving over and over again the first night Dr. Sanchez and I had been…intimate…I knew that this drug was going to change everything.

Dr. Sanchez

When the mainstream media linked Dream to my lab, hundreds of politicians and weekend scientists stepped forward overnight, accusing me of developing Dream for the sole purpose of creating addicts from whom I could profit. Nothing is further from the truth. I truly hoped to develop something that could help people sleep. That was it. Frankly, it was rather insulting that people thought I was making a profit from Dream. I wasn't. It was Megan Winters and all the people who were reproducing the drug and selling it who were making money. It was despicable, really.

Edison Chin, Chief of the New York City Police Department

Many blamed the NYPD for the Dream epidemic, implying that if we had been able to stop it sooner, it never would have reached the level of pervasiveness that it did. But that is too simple an explanation. When Dream first hit the streets, people were rather ambivalent about it, comparing it to Valium or Ritalin. And the class components were obvious— no one wanted the NYPD busting into the homes of rich doctors and lawyers while they were enjoying a sweet dream. What on Earth were we supposed to do?

Tony Williams

I firmly believe that I lost my bid for reelection as mayor of New York because I took a tough stance against Dream. With all the other issues the city was facing—rising housing costs, a dilapidated public transit system, intermittent flooding—no one wanted resources directed to addressing an epidemic that for many was not doing any harm. Many stopped me on the sidewalk, asking me what I had against people who slept. If people were willing to protest over the drug, shouldn't people, especially the federal government, have known that something was wrong? That maybe Dream was different?

Miles Lattimore

While I had known that Dream was going to be lucrative, when Megan first approached me to distribute the stuff, I had no idea how lucrative it was going to be. I initially wanted to have access to it for myself, but when dealers began fighting with each other—literally pulling knives and guns on one another—to get access to product, I knew that I had to be more than Megan's middleman.

Megan Winters

I never should have trusted Miles. I knew exactly what he was doing when he asked to learn how to produce Dream. When I refused, he came back using language straight out of a business school textbook, as if he was presenting some novel idea. Deep down, however, I think my subconscious just really wanted to stick it to Dr. Sanchez.

Miles Lattimore

I was shocked when Megan gave me the formula. I thought I was going to have to coerce her, possibly woo her romantically. As someone who was used to doing everything in his power for a fix, I had been prepared to do anything to find out how to make it. Absolutely anything.

Stanley Larkin, Best Friend of Miles Lattimore

The first time Miles gave me Dream, I was highly skeptical. It didn't make any sense—if a drug really existed that could make you control your dreams, reliving, and more importantly, re-experiencing any moment you wished, how come the drug was not all over the place? Supply and demand, he said; it was too hard to get the drug, so most people thought it was an urban legend. When I woke up from that first hit, I knew that this was something special. I told Miles that he had to do whatever it took to get the formula. When he came back and explained it could be made with a high school chemistry kit and some items you could pick up at a local pharmacy, I knew that we were in business.

Commissioner Chin

The reason why we at the NYPD were so slow to react to the proliferation of Dream was how it was being distributed: college students. The largest distributors in the city were kids living in dorm rooms at Columbia and NYU. I guess that none of us made that obvious connection, that a drug developed at Cornell would subsequently be distributed at other universities.

Dr. Sanchez

People claimed that Dream spread from college campuses, but the truth is that its popularity didn't truly skyrocket until J.D. Smythe, backup point guard for the Knicks, started using it. He had long had issues sleeping, along with anxiety caused by the stresses that came with being a professional basketball player. When he went on ESPN and credited the sudden turnaround in his career to Dream—he went from journeyman to Sixth Man of the Year candidate—I wanted to cheer and groan at the same time.

J.D. Smythe, New York Knick

My girlfriend was in her first year of residency when she told me about this drug people were taking that was better than an alarm clock and helped them study. One of her attendings said that she used Dream to study for 45 minutes while she napped every day, going over surgical techniques and the like while her body rested. When my girlfriend said that I could visualize my shooting stroke while I slept, I knew that I had to at least try it. I, along with my agent, was so glad I did.

Stanley Larkin

Not a lot of people knew who J.D. Smythe was before he won Most Improved Player and Sixth Man of the Year, but I did. He did me the honor of telling the world that it was his girlfriend that introduced Dream to him, but it was really me, his high school buddy, who gave him the hookup. Last thing I wanted was the police looking into me. Besides, J.D. owed me. Not only was his game better, but he became one of the most popular players in the NBA (not because he was a good guy, but because he could hook anyone up with Dream).

Sarah Johnson, President of the United States

By the time I was elected, drug crises and epidemics had taken a back seat to gun control, abortion, and the economy. It was just not something that the Executive Branch typically had to deal with. That all changed when the military began reporting issues of extensive Dream use. Soldiers were using all their free time to sleep, and many used any excuse possible to skip active duty, feigning sickness or injury.

At that point, Dream became my problem.

Brad Hussein, Surgeon General of the United States

When my various contacts abroad started asking whether I could speed up the FDA's review of Dream, I knew that trouble was brewing. I had not even been aware that the drug was under review. I had only heard about it in on the local news, something no different than when I had to field calls from parents at my daughter's school after someone saw a feature about the dangers of wheat or why children should not be eating food after 7 p.m.

J.D. Smythe

When the NBA, along with every other professional league, added Dream to the list of banned substances, I wanted to die. Literally. I mean, over half the NBA smoked weed. Just leave us alone. It's not like Dream made us get bigger like steroids. It didn't make us do stupid shit. It helped us sleep. And for all those people who said it was like a mental steroid, come on. Was it any different than paying a sport's psychologist? It was certainly cheaper.

Dr. Sanchez

Even though I received a number of high-profile grants after Dream was traced back to my lab, I never received the call that all underpaid researchers hoped for: a big pharmaceutical company inviting me to come aboard. The tension that existed was understandable. Venture capital funds and even government agencies were interested in providing grant money for future projects and breakthroughs, but large pharmaceutical companies—those with real money—were hesitant to hire me, as if their shareholders would object to having a leading drug designer on their payroll.

Lindsey Lam

I didn't understand Dr. Sanchez's burning desire to be absorbed by a giant pharmaceutical company and leave an educational institution like Cornell. Did he really think that we would make more money that way? Have access to more resources? Everyone who I knew that made that kind of jump regretted it. As much as I respected Dr. Sanchez, I did not think that he would be able to give away the autonomy and control that he enjoyed running his own lab.

Henry Contiff, Commissioner of the U.S. Food and Drug Administration

When I received the call from President Johnson asking my thoughts on Dream, I was embarrassed to admit that I was a secret user. My wife died a few years ago and I had heard that the drug would allow me to relive my favorite moments with her. The last thing I wanted was for the FDA to review the drug for fear we would be forced to denounce or ban it. It was hard enough getting a hold of Dream as it was.

President Johnson

If we had control of the House and Senate, I guarantee that things would have gone differently. As it was, it was impossible to pass any federal legislation curtailing or restricting the use of Dream. If people thought the NRA was a powerful interest group, think again. Proponents of Dream were the single most powerful interest group that I, or any other President before me, had ever encountered. People seemed to think that the right to get high and sleep was as sacred as the right to bear arms.

Dr. Sanchez

Testifying before the Senate was something I never thought I would have to do. When I was initially invited, I "pretended" not to have received the email. Usually if someone misses an email, you receive a gentle reminder or follow-up email. People receive hundreds of emails a day. I learned quickly that ignoring an email from the U.S. Senate was not something to do, especially when they beckoned you.

Margo Stein, Chairperson of the U.S. Senate Emergency Subcommittee on Dream

I was absolutely appalled by the sheer lack of guilt and regret coming from Dr. Sanchez as he sat there and parroted over and over again the same refrain: "I had no idea what we had on our hands." Either he was lying or he was completely incompetent. He had published dozens of articles on the drug, discussing all its potential uses, and now he was claiming he had no idea what it did? Preposterous.

President Johnson

If only someone had taken the time to prepare Dr. Sanchez for his testimony. Did he think he was going to have a lovely conversation with people who wanted to bask in his genius? The media had a field day vilifying him. But his lack of foresight was not the real problem. The real problem was that, whether he did it on purpose or not, he revealed to the world how to create the drug. Anyone with any knowledge of chemistry could figure out how to produce the drug with a little experimentation.

Henry Contiff

I was flabbergasted as I listened to Dr. Sanchez's testimony. Here was a man with degrees from Harvard and Cambridge who did did not stop to think that maybe, just maybe, testifying before a Senate Committee at a public hearing was not the place to discuss how "elegantly simple" the drug was to make. Did he think that would insulate him in some way from liability?

Megan Winters

Truthfully, when Dr. Sanchez shared the chemical structure of Dream I was floored. I did not think he knew what it was. I really was pleasantly surprised. I guess he may have been more than just a physicist.

Stanley Larkin

I'm not one to pay attention to grandstanding politicians. Frankly, I can't tell the difference between a Democrat, Republican, Socialist, or a Fascist. But I do pay attention when political hacks are messing with my business. When Dr. Sanchez spilled the beans on national television—okay, CSPAN wasn't really national television, but people did watch it from time to time—I knew that I had to start churning out and selling as much Dream as I could. It was my last chance to make some money before the price hit rock bottom because anyone could make it.

Commissioner Chin

If the NYPD and, frankly, every other police department thought they had problems with Dream before, within a month of Dr. Sanchez's infamous testimony, it was impossible to contain the epidemic. Every major news outlet, from CNN to *The New York Times* to *The Huffington Post*, ran stories of journalists describing their attempts to recreate the drug, as if cracking the perfect form of Dream were no different than cracking the recipe for the frosting of a Magnolia cupcake.

Ultimately, none of this would have mattered if people were not so addicted to the drug. Being addicted to Dream would not have been much of a problem for us if every ten minutes we weren't receiving a 911 call with someone frantically reporting a missing person. People weren't missing. They were sleeping.

Lindsey Lam

Other than Dream's highly addictive nature, Dream had no detrimental effects. That was part of what made the drug so incredible. It did exactly what it said it would, allowed people to sleep as needed, with the added benefit of having people truly enjoy that sleep. I think that's why it took so long for the authorities to come down on us.

President Johnson

When the economy's stagnation was indirectly linked to a sharp decrease in total employee labor hours, and that in turn was linked, both directly and indirectly, to the steady rise of the use of Dream, I would have thought Republicans and fiscal conservatives would have come pouring out, looking for legislation outlawing the drug. Unfortunately, as I would only learn later, 60% of the Senate and 73% of the House were Dream users. I had feared that various interest groups had found a clandestine way to buy our representatives. Instead, it was the representatives themselves who were allowing Dream to lead the country into ruin.

J.D. Smythe

When I received the summons from the White House—The WHITE HOUSE—I cursed myself. I should have learned from the experiences of Mark McGwire and Jose Conseco. Hell, I should have taken a page out of Lance Armstrong's book and never told anybody that I was using Dream. Then I could have had years of success like Lance. And if things went wrong, I would have hopefully squirreled away enough money so that it wouldn't matter if they kicked me out of the league or vilified me for using an illegal substance to get ahead.

President Johnson

No one could give me an alternative to what my Chief of Staff had dubbed "The Poison Pill." Some estimated that two in three people had taken Dream and that one in two people was addicted to Dream. The economy was tanking; our military, unbeknownst to our enemies, was struggling to protect our interests at home and abroad; and no one seemed to be able to create an effective antidote.

When I made the call and signed the secret Executive Order, I did so doing what I was tasked to do, as the President of the United States of America. Many thought that I was overstepping my authority, going beyond what the Constitution had intended, but in the weeks and months after the announcement, I was vindicated. Millions may have cursed my name, but I knew that, in time, my name would be spoken with the same reverence as George Washington and Abraham Lincoln.

Commissioner Chin

I, along with everyone else in the Department, was shocked when we watched President Johnson make the announcement. We had received word that we were going to be given the green light on Operation Zombie 48 hours before the announcement so that we could prepare making sweeps and arresting known users. The problem, which the President had acknowledged in the memo, was that we also had to detain those in the force who were using. I knew that once officers heard that we would be drug-testing our own, implementing the President's directive would be a challenge.

Kyle Reese, Captain in the NYPD

If I had known that testing positive for using Dream was going to get me sent to a detention center, I never would have agreed to pee in that damn cup. I wish I had the chance to warn everyone I knew, but the people upstairs had been smart enough to take people into custody the moment the liquid in the cup turned purple.

Dr. Sanchez

I was already on a plane bound for Hong Kong when President Johnson made her stunning announcement. I had been tipped off a day earlier by a friend in the White House, that I ought to grab my loved ones and anyone in the lab I that valued and get out of the country. When I landed, and saw every television set at the airport covering what was happening back in the U.S., I was glad to have been lucky enough to get out of there.

Megan Winters

I was shocked when the Ithaca police came knocking at my door and asked to test me to see if I was a Dream user. How stupid did they think I was? I helped develop the drug. Unlike Lindsey, who I knew had been taking the drug regularly "in the name of science," I was not going to put Dream into my body. I saw how dependent people became and I wanted none of it.

What really bothered me was that after I passed the drug test, the officers asked me if I knew where Dr. Sanchez was. You mean he wasn't home? He wasn't hijacking some panel about the benefits of research? How was I supposed to know?

Stanley Larkin

When I found out that J.D. had killed himself rather than be detained, I wondered whether I should do the same thing. I knew that I had a little more time before they came for me, as the first people they had gone after were those in the media who had admitted to using Dream or anyone who had long advocated for its use. The question was whether I was willing to take my chances going into hiding and wait for authorities to inevitably find me, or to join J.D. in finding out whether there was an afterlife.

J.D. Smythe

I couldn't do it. I just couldn't. The idea that they were going to take Dream away from me? Make me live in a detention facility? What was this? Trying to send us to a gulag or concentration camp? We all know how those things went. I couldn't do it. So I did what I think many decided to do—I took as much Dream as possible, hoping that I could stay asleep forever.

President Johnson

When I authorized "The Poison Pill," I had not thought of the possibility that it would encourage hundreds of thousands of people to overdose on Dream as a way of escaping detention. The numbers were truly astonishing and it would take decades for the population to recover. If I had known how high the number of suicides would be, I would have waited to find some other solution.

Dr. Hussein

I had warned the President that she should not go down this road. The toll on individuals was unknown and no one really knew what the outcome would be. The report we provided to the President outlined the potential outcomes, including the possibility that a large segment of the affected population would commit suicide. The problem was, of course, was that to heed our warnings, she would have had to read the report. Unfortunately, as with so many reports that crossed her desk, she did not.

Lindsey Lam

I had not been to Hong Kong for more a decade when Dr. Sanchez and I arrived. I feared that at any moment, someone would show up at our door, throw hoods over our head, and extradite us back to the United States. Luckily, that never happened. I should have known that Dr. Sanchez would have a plan.

Dr. Sanchez

To think that it would be the Chinese government that would be the ones to appreciate my genius. Lindsey was apprehensive, and yes, we could never return to the United States, but we were also now being compensated at a level worthy of our skill. It may not have been a dream come true, but it was certainly something to be proud of.

The Seven-Year Flood

Year 7

We spent almost every day that summer digging trenches and building a wall made out of sandbags, as if a thirty-five-year-old single father and his eight-year-old and six-year-old children could build something that could keep an ocean at bay. My father believed that, armed with $250 worth of supplies, two shovels, and some old-fashioned grit and determination, the three of us could do something that the island's leading real estate developer had offered to do for $50,000.

"$50,000, Dan? For what? All I want is a flood wall and a trench so that we don't have to wake up one morning to find our kitchen flooded."

My parents had purchased our house on a lark. An uncle on my mother's side sold them on the idea that once they had children, they would want nothing more than to have a place to escape with their children—and then, when their children were too old for "family vacations," a place where they could escape to enjoy themselves. The house would mean there was never a debate over where to go for a vacation, no need to scour the internet for cheap hotels. When my mother died, with us having only spent one week over four years in our so-called "vacation paradise," my father decided that he had had enough of renting the house to other people to enjoy and that it was time for us to enjoy it.

Permanently.

And just like that, we were no longer New Yorkers. I was four and my sister was two when we packed up our things and said goodbye to what we now referred to as the Mainland.

Those first few days that summer of manual labour were fun, as it was easy to let our imaginations take over. It was a game, an extended recess, our minds happy to be free from the shackles of school. Under the relentless summer sun, as we dug that trench and built that flood wall, we imagined that we were preparing fortifications to repel oncoming invaders. We were building a castle wall, something stronger and more impenetrable than the walls of Helm's Deep in *The Two Towers* or The Wall from *Game of Thrones*. We were re-enacting battles from World War I. These were but a few of the many fantasies we played out while we went about the repetitive process of filling bags with the sand we were digging up from our trench. Unfortunately, there is only so much an overactive imagination can mask. By the end of the fourth day, there was nothing that my sister or I wanted to do more than sleep.

Our father had a different idea.

"How can you both be tired? If you're tired now, we're never going to finish. When I was your age, I was already bussing tables at Meredith's."

Our father thought that berating us and pointing out how much easier we had it than him would make us work harder. Instead, it only increased our resentment. Our friends, whose homes were facing similar encroachment by the ocean, were busy doing what children living on an island paradise had always done—running along the beach, swimming in the ocean, or, simply, enjoying life. And even though Stacey and I were young, we were old enough to see the major flaw in our father's tales of underage employment. If he had really been bussing tables at the island's oldest and most popular restaurant (which was hard to believe because all of Meredith's wait staff were related to Meredith in some way), our father was getting *paid* to do it. No one was paying us for our labor under the hot summer sun. But even though Stacey and I soon grew to harbor deep resentment for the work, neither of us complained. We knew that if we did, we would lose what little allowance money our father gave us each week.

By the end of that summer, after seeing how little our makeshift wall and shallow trench was doing to repel the ever-creeping tide—we had to move back our so-called last stand multiple times because the water was creeping up too quickly—our father decided to abandon the project. Rather than fight the inevitable, he decided we needed to find another way to hold back the tide.

Year 6

"What do you mean you're moving? Where on Earth are you going to go?" my father asked angrily.

"Back to Beijing. Anywhere that's not surrounded by water," Bernie, our long-time neighbor replied.

"Everywhere is surrounded by water," my father exclaimed, before storming off.

For years, people had been slowly leaving the island. At first, it was barely noticeable, mostly rich celebrities or snowbirds who skipped a winter or two. People would ask, "Where are Ken and Barbara?" or "Did the Wests not come out this year?" When "For Sale" signs started popping up in front of the more expensive properties, people started speculating as to which movie star or hedge fund manager was going to move in. But few, if any, of those properties were ever sold, and those "For Sale" signs remained, a permanent reminder that those houses, once looked upon with envy by tourists and residents alike, were no longer inhabited by those they envied.

Our father spent much of that year looking into how to literally pick up our house and move it back from the beach a hundred feet. He had been reading about the wealthy in Miami buying up once less desirable property farther from the coastline in anticipation of rising sea levels and ever-bigger tropical storms. Purchasing property farther inland was not an issue for us—we already owned it, as our property went from the coastline all the way back to the single road connecting us to the capital. However, if we could not afford $50,000 for a flood wall, we were not going to be able to afford $100,000 to pick up and move our house back 100 feet. Neither my sister nor myself understood the magnitude of the project—why not simply get a crane to life our house from one spot to another? Our failed wall and trench had done little to curb our imagination or help us understand how difficult a task holding onto our house would be.

It was not until our friends Tom and Trip, twins who lived a mile away, came to say goodbye that Stacey and I started to wonder whether we should move too. Maybe flooding was inevitable.

Our father would hear none of it.

"This is our home. We are not leaving," he said, not even taking the time to look up from his newspaper. "Where would we go?"

"Tom and Trip are moving to Australia," I replied, not understanding the question was rhetorical. Not realizing his silence was not an invitation to keep talking, I went on. "Everybody is leaving. We're just being stupid by staying here."

When my father put down the newspaper, I knew I had said something I should not have. But instead of a tongue-lashing, my father simply stood up and headed back to his bedroom, closing the door behind him.

"Uh oh," Stacey whispered.

"You're telling me."

Year 5

Just an hour before our reservation to play mini golf to celebrate Stacey's eighth birthday, we found ourselves, along with a dozen other families, cramped in our living room watching a broadcast of our president, Susan Coombs, addressing (begging, really) the United Nations to do something about global warming and climate change. Dressed in a charcoal suit, a pair of glasses perched atop her nose, she looked nothing like the woman everyone called Island Mom. I had never seen her in anything other than brightly-colored dresses.

"What a waste of time. Nothing is going to happen," Beth, one of the Island's three kindergarten teachers said. "They barely do anything for their own people. Look at what the U.S. did after Hurricane Katrina and Hurricane Maria."

"Have faith," my father said.

"Since when did you believe in God?" Beth asked.

"Who said anything about God?" my father replied. "If there were a God, would He or She or It allow for this to be happening? Look out that window. Look at all that water that has been creeping up for years. In a year, it'll be at our back porch. If there were a God, would God let us all drown? No, when I say faith, I have faith in Susan."

Stacey and I, like our father, had faith that Island Mom would convince the United Nations to save us. The only question was how. Would they build the giant wall that we had been unable to, cover the Island in a giant dome, or raise the Island on stilts? Or maybe they would fly us to another island, one that was so tall that the ocean would never be able to reclaim it.

It was because of everyone's faith that Island Mom would be successful—regardless of the many that had failed before her—that everyone was crammed into our living room watching the telecast. Stacey was especially annoyed that this was ruining her birthday. She thought that if we did not leave soon, our reservation at Bianca's Mini-Golf would be cancelled. I doubted there were so many people that wanted to play mini golf on a Wednesday night that our reservation would be cancelled (especially because most people who called the Island home were glued to their televisions like us), but I knew that if I said anything, Stacey would have cried.

When Island Mom finally finished her remarks and was subsequently showered in applause, Stacey was fast asleep and all I wanted to do was eat. My father and the other adults present seemed buoyed from the response from the U.N. delegates from around the world. It looked as if Island Mom had come through as expected.

"I knew that there was a reason why I always voted for her," my father said. "I had my doubts. I mean, the Island is already 10% under water. Let's just hope that the rest of the world realizes we need help. Maybe people are paying attention now." My father threw on his golf visor and smiled. "Okay, Stacey, ready to beat your old man?"

"She's asleep," I replied, stifling a yawn.

Everyone laughed.

"That's too bad. I was looking forward to getting some hole-in-ones."

"We can wake her up," I said.

"No, it's her birthday. Let her sleep. We can play mini-golf another day."

Unfortunately, we would never get that chance. A few weeks later, we found out that the owners of Bianca's Mini-Golf had packed up their things and moved to Australia.

Year 4

Although the Island's tourist industry seemed relatively immune to the ever-encroaching waters, it was during the off-peak months, especially during the rainy season, when us locals began noticing the changes. When Marty, the owner of three convenience stores on the Island, wanted to charge $5 for a Mars Bar, alarm bells went off in my head.

"$5? Marty, you're gonna charge my kid $5 for a candy bar?" my father asked, waving the candy bar in Marty's face.

"Look, you know I love you and your family, but it's not like we're getting hundreds of these a week anymore like we used to. I'm getting a box of 48 of these every 6 months."

"It's just one bar for my kid."

"I can't. I have to save these for the tourists who can afford whatever price I set. I have to make some money off of these things."

"Come kids, let's get out of here. Let's find someone who isn't going to extort loyal customers over a chocolate bar."

"What's extortion?" Stacey asked as we walked out.

"It's not what your father thinks it means," Marty sighed.

"Well, it sure as hell doesn't matter what it means, now does it?" my father said angrily.

As we walked out of the store, our heads bowed, we knew that finding another place to buy our chocolate bars was not going to be easy. We could drive 30 minutes to the capital, but that was excessive, especially considering the price of gas had gone up faster than the price of a Mars bar (and even if gas prices had not gone up, driving 30 minutes for a chocolate bar was definitely excessive). The only other places close to us were the hotel gift shops down the road, but those were for suckers. The wide assortment of candy was specifically chosen for tourists because they had learned long ago that those who could afford to fly to the Island and stay in an expensive hotel could afford to pay for over-priced bags of chips and other things that reminded them of home. We mocked these tourists for their wastefulness and lack of foresight. Why not have just packed those things in their luggage? However, no matter how stupid we thought those tourists were, we would all trade places with them if given the chance. They had access to so many things, including Amazon, which was still a sore spot for us as their version of express shipping meant an order would arrive within two weeks.

For four months after the dustup with Marty, we did not set foot in any of his stores. It was strange—we used to visit almost every day, picking up something as small as a roll of toilet paper. Instead, once a week we piled into our beat-up Volkswagen Bug and drove 30 minutes to the capital to buy groceries and other supplies, something we used to do only once a month. We enjoyed the trips, and having the chance to wander streets where we did not know everyone made me wonder what it would be like to wander around a real city like London or Tokyo. However, every time I bit into a chocolate bar, I thought about all the discounts and free things Marty used to give us. He was always kind and I wondered whether he noticed our absences.

Seventeen weeks after the Mars Bar incident, we came home to find a small package addressed to Stacey and me by our door. Inside was a box of 48 Mars Bars and a note—"Sorry for everything. Closing up the shops because I couldn't find people to buy $5 chocolate bars. I hope you enjoy them."

Year 3

"Everyone, please calm down. There's no reason to panic," Island Mom said from the podium.

"Why should we panic?" one person yelled. "It was one thing when it was just flooding, but now we have to deal with never-ending rain? Our freshwater is being polluted with salt water and you're telling us not to panic?"

As the person continued, more voices spoke up.

"Please, calm down," Island Mom said. "We have been preparing for this. Everything will be all right."

"Maybe for you. You're rich and can fly out of here tomorrow, but what about the rest of us?" someone yelled.

"Come on," my father said. "Let's go."

We followed him out of the hall, the chorus of people growing louder and louder. While most of the adults were concerned about freshwater reserves and preserving the wildlife, all the children, like us, were excited. After the accelerated flooding reclaimed the beaches, the waters started to reclaim the swimming pools and water parks dotting the coastline. These spaces had been closed off to us our whole lives, our only encounters consisting of us looking longingly at the tourists going down the slides and doing cannonballs into the giant pools. When we voiced our envy to our father, he would dismiss us.

"Why do you need a pool? We have the ocean. Those parents and children envy us."

As the smaller hotels started to close and the larger ones realized that the cost of maintaining their pools and water parks was too much, they started thinking like my father— why have a pool if the ocean was a dozen yards away. Luckily for us, rather than break down those slides or board up the pools, they simply left them alone, not wanting to incur any more costs with the money sucks. This meant we now had free reign to enjoy the things that had been off-limits to us for so long. We used the water slides and swam lengths in the pools. No, it was not the same, as it was now ocean and rainwater instead of clear heavily chlorinated water, but we enjoyed it nonetheless.

Even now, decades later, enjoying those abandoned pools were still some of the best moments of my life.

Year 2

After school ended for that year—and by school, literally school as a concept, as there was only one left on the island—

we spent the summer hanging out in some of the abandoned hotels. While the Island never experienced any super storms, we continued to experience bouts of rain that would last 24 to 48 hours, which left large parts of the Island flooded for days. We had been forced to abandon our home and rent a small apartment in the capital. My father complained that it was highway robbery, but deep down we suspected he understood how lucky we were to find a place at all.

"Look kids, all we have to do is hold out. The United Nations is going to come through. Just you wait."

Neither Stacey nor I wanted to burst his bubble. He believed that staying was better than leaving. His optimism was not completely unfounded—the United Nations had designated the Island as one of five places where they would test various methods to fight global warning. They had even flown out Leonardo DiCaprio for a press conference. On our Island, they were testing floodwalls of all kinds and while Island Mom asked people to temper their expectations, many, including my father, were certain things were going to turn around.

While the adults debated the future, all of us kids continued to enjoy greater access to more spaces than ever before. We loved the abandoned hotels the most. We spent many days exploring these once majestic buildings. If our imaginations ran wild years ago while building walls and digging trenches, we were truly free in the ghost hotels. We ran around playing hide-and-go-seek, oblivious to the fact that if we got hurt, it could be fatal because most roads to those hotels were underwater.

If we weren't expected home each night, I'm certain we all would have taken up residence in those abandoned hotels. We did worry, however, that the water would get so deep that we would not be able to get to the hotels any longer.

That time would come much sooner than we thought.

Year 1

The emergency evacuation center was set up at the northern end of the Island where tourists used to take stunning cliffside photos. Had the center been set up a decade ago, it would not have been able to hold the 10,000 people who called the Island home. But because the population had dropped to 1,500, there was plenty of space for the 500 who had been displaced, with the remaining 1,000 vowing to "fight the good fight." My father decided that even though our rental was still habitable, we would be higher on the waiting list for transport off the Island if we relocated to the evacuation center. With the airport having been flooded for good a year ago, the only way off the Island was by ship—and if you could not afford to pay for a spot (and if you did, you would have left years ago), you were at the mercy of the single United Nations vessel that relocated people to Australia or Hawaii. Most wanted Hawaii because they thought the U.S. would never let anything happen to those islands, but I saw little logic in going from a flood zone to a potential flood zone.

What was most tragic was that we were now confined to certain areas of the Island while waiting for rescue. There were a few abandoned hotels we could wander through, but without access to a boat, we could not enjoy the places we once roamed freely. We thought we could build one using discarded wood and debris, but we soon learned that building a useable craft took more time than any of us wanted to invest. At one point, we saved enough to buy a beat-up fishing trawler, only to wake up and learn it had been stolen. We thought that given the Island's dwindling population, authorities would hunt down the thieves with ease. That would assume we had a functioning police force or coast guard, which we had not had for years. If we had been more observant, we would have realized no one was stopping us from wandering around various abandoned buildings, especially since it was all still technically private property.

After three weeks of living in the camp, we learned that we were going to be evacuated on the next ship to Hawaii, where we could stay in a converted hotel for up to six months. Stacey wanted to stay in Hawaii, a chance to continue Island life; I liked the idea but feared any island we went to would share the same fate as our home. And even worse, Hawaii had volcanoes. Instead, I wanted to move to the middle of Africa, far away from any ocean. Ultimately, it did not matter what we wanted, as our father had his own plan.

"We're going to live in Hawaii and live in that hotel until they kick us out. When they do, we're going to come back here where we belong."

Stacey loved the idea, thinking of Hawaii as a vacation.

Was I the only one in my family that was not crazy?

It was surreal, watching the time-lapsed footage of the Island—our Island—being reclaimed by the waters from whence it sprung. CNN had done a feature on "Extreme Climate Change," which we watched, riveted, as scientists discussed the inevitable flooding of almost every low-lying area across the globe. They warned it was a question of "if," not "when." On good nights, my father would simply shake his head when he thought of the Island, now 78% underwater. However, if he had been drinking, he would spend his time yelling at the sky, asking why this happened to us.

"If it had been New York City, you'd see people handle things differently," he would say to us or anyone listening.

The irony was that he was often saying this in our tiny 22nd floor apartment on 95th and 3rd in Manhattan. After spending eight months in Hawaii, he decided to take us back to where it all started. While Manhattan was yet another island dealing with its own climate change-related issues, my father firmly believed this island would never truly be in danger.

"There is too much money here for people to let anything to happen to us," he said.

Neither Stacey nor I said anything, but I wanted to remind him, "That's what you said about our Island, that the rich celebrities would not let anything happen. Too bad you can't reason with Mother Nature."

But I never said anything. I knew it was not worth it— why fight the inevitable. Instead, I would hunker down on the couch, waiting until my father got bored with the news until I could change the channel and watch something else.

Alphabetica: The Other Side of Love

Animosity (noun)

There were times you told me that I treated you like a hostile witness taking the stand. That I said whatever it took to get a rise out of you, as if I actually *enjoyed* the fighting that always ended in tears. Sometimes, but not often, you were right. Sometimes, when a client did something stupid or a judgment did not go my way, I did come home in a foul mood, looking to pick a fight. On those occasions, I did want to fight with someone until I could confidently say that I was the victor. Your tears were a sign of my victory. Other times—most of the time—I just wanted you to listen to what I had to say instead of being your usual, stubborn self, refusing to relent until you not only got your way, but got me to admit to the wrongness of mine. Those were the times when I did not want to fight but was prepared to. When those fights ended in tears, no one won.

Bristol Board (noun)

The store had so many different colors. This was not a Rite Aid, Duane Reade, or Walgreens. Instead of blue, the store carried periwinkle, baby blue, ultramarine, neon blue, and navy.

Maria could not decide which one she wanted to use for her sixth-grade science fair project, so you told her that she could have one of each. I shook my head, knowing that it was a waste and that we could not afford it. Besides, how many of the oversized pieces of paper would end up in the recycling? Even the ones she used for her display would find their way to a recycling plant after the science fair.

When I told Maria that she could only choose two colors, she got angry and sulked.

"Mommy said I could get one of each."

It was times like these that explain why she chose to live with you instead of me.

Chocolate (noun)

My nightstand was always empty, but yours always had a book and a chocolate bar resting on it. You said the chocolate was in case of an emergency, in case you got hungry in the middle of the night. You never ate it. Instead, every so often, you would throw the current one out and replace it with a new one.

One night, while you were out watching a movie with your girlfriends, I came home drunk and ate the Snickers bar that you had left earlier that morning. I left the wrapper on the nightstand and fell asleep. When I woke up the next morning, the wrapper was gone. You did not say a word.

You never left a chocolate bar on your nightstand again.

Dance (noun; verb)

I had always wanted to learn how to ballroom dance, so when I found out that the nearby community college was offering free classes on Wednesday nights, I signed us up immediately. I thought it would be a great opportunity for us to do something together, to enjoy each other's company the way we used to when we had first started dating. The first time we went, you had such a blast that you blocked off an hour each night so that we could practice. You thought it was important to show our teacher that we were making progress and taking the class seriously while all the other couples in the class showed little to no improvement from week to week. While I pretended that those evening practices were a burden, deep down I was just as excited for them. I left work looking forward to guiding you around our small living room. Those months were probably the happiest that we had during our marriage.

Six months in, you got pregnant. We kept going, but after a while, your feet started to swell and you had to cancel our evening practices. Once you started to show, you became too self-conscious in the class's makeshift studio to enjoy yourself. Because I could not hold you closely in the same way, you felt as if everyone in the class was watching you. No one ever was.

When we finally stopped going, I understood. But you felt like you were letting me down. You told me to keep going, but I couldn't. It just wouldn't have been the same without you.

Envy (noun; verb)

Enrolling Maria in a private school was a mistake. Every day she came home wanting something one of her classmates had—Malibu Barbie, pink sneakers, a Hello Kitty watch, a Kate Spade pencil case. When she started asking questions about Coach, Dior, and Prada, I pitied all the people who were one day going to fall in love with her.

You told Maria that one day, when Daddy became a big-shot lawyer, he would buy you all those things. Until then, you told her that she should be grateful for everything she had. She was so much more fortunate than other children.

After a week of listening to Maria sigh whenever she told us about all the things that her classmates who were even more fortunate than her brought to school, I set aside enough money to buy Maria the pink sneakers she had been going on and on about. I was so excited to see the look on her face. But when I gave them to her, she cried. They were a half size too small.

"You bought her shoes without first checking her size?"

You did not talk to me for the rest of the night.

Facebook (noun)

I hated everything to do with social networks. They were all the same to me. I was not one of the hundreds of millions of people that Mark Zuckerberg was able to make millions off of by tapping into a deep-seated need to share their lives with others.

You, on the other hand, were the exact opposite. You publicized our whole relationship. You updated your status, added pictures, and put up Shakespearean quotes that you thought described how we felt about one another. If something of interest happened between us, hundreds of people knew about it within minutes of its occurrence. In fact, all your so-called "friends" knew that we were engaged before I had a chance to tell my parents that you had said "yes."

You continued to update your account even after we got married. You had fun putting up pictures of our honeymoon, our first apartment, and baby pictures of Maria, even though I was uncomfortable with you putting pictures of her up online. Whose business was any of this anyway?

When I finally signed the papers and got around to contacting some of our mutual friends to let them know what had happened, they already knew. Apparently, you had been "single" for a month already.

Girlfriend (noun)

The first time I introduced you to my parents, I simply said, "This is Amanda." You did not tell me until we got back to my apartment that I was supposed to introduce you with something more elaborate than just your name. You said that you were hurt because you always introduced me to your friends by saying "Hi, this is my boyfriend, Carlos." I did not respond because I could see how upset you were, but I wondered if it could somehow be unclear to my parents that I was dating you given that I had arranged the meeting at their insistence.

Hickey (noun)

I thought it was funny, the way you were so angry at me the next morning. All I could do was laugh as you rummaged through all your silk scarves in order to find something to throw on. When I suggested a turtleneck, you sneered. There was no way you were going to wear a turtleneck in 90-degree weather. You called me so many different things—childish, inconsiderate, stupid, a buffoon—but all it did was make me laugh even harder. By the time you were done stomping around and huffing and puffing, all you could do was smile at me and pull me close to you.

"Why should I be the only one who has to deal with this?" you asked, before pushing me back onto the bed.

If (conjunction)

For a long time, all I wanted to do was go back in time to *that* night and make sure we never met. I had wanted to skip the office holiday party altogether because I had a deposition the next morning. But my secretary said that I worked too hard and that everyone had to take a break once in a while. It was the holidays—even the partners were taking the night off.

When I got to the party, everyone had brought their significant others, so I immediately felt out of place. I had told Leslie, the girl I had been casually seeing at the time, that the party was for employees only. Besides, the last thing I wanted was for my coworkers to see me show up with a girl who had purple and green streaks in her hair and a tattoo of Speed Racer on her forearm.

Luckily, you were there, standing by the finger sandwiches, seeming just as out of place as I did. I assumed that you worked in a different department and, like me, was wondering when would be a good time to slip back to the office.

How was I supposed to know that you, a cute brunette who seemed like she actually enjoyed my conversation, would be the source of so much joy followed by so much grief?

Well, for starters, I probably should have realized that you were someone's guest as soon as I found out you did not work at the firm. And I should have realized that the man who took you aside and screamed at you for fifteen minutes was probably not just a friend but was actually the guy who you later told me that you had been dating for three years before you started dating me.

If only I had not been so instantly smitten with you, I would have been able to avoid all the things that followed.

Jazz (noun)

When you talked about it, I could not help but think about how pretentious you sounded. You argued that scat and the blues were the natural evolution of opera and the fugue, as if all music originated from the same starting point, the first human beings banging on a cave wall or communicating in the earliest form of song. All I could do was nod my head whenever you went on one of your music rants because none of it was music I cared for. If it was not music that you would expect to hear at a Super Bowl halftime show, then I didn't really care for it. While your friends lamented the state of popular music and "all that crap on the radio," I was more than willing to immediately go to iTunes and buy a catchy song I had just heard on Z100. As far as I was concerned, there was a reason that it was called "popular music"—it was good.

The only time that I ever voiced my opinion on the matter, using your arguments and stating that Kelly Clarkson and Miley Cyrus were the natural evolution of Miles Davis and John Coltrane, you picked up my copy of the Hannah Montana soundtrack and snapped it in two.

I learned then never to argue with you about the things that you loved.

Karate (noun)

When Maria asked if she could learn karate, I thought it was a great idea. A young girl would soon grow up to be a young woman, and a young woman needed to be able to protect herself. You were hesitant at first because you were afraid that she would get hurt, but after some extensive discussions (and begging on Maria's part), you finally relented. Maybe it would be a good idea for her to learn how to defend herself, especially if she was going to start taking the subway home from school by herself. As the first class approached, you became even more excited than Maria, even going so far as to look into signing up for classes yourself.

After the second day of class, Maria came back with a broken wrist.

You shook your head and said, "I told you so," as if you had been against the idea all along.

Love (noun; verb)

I thought that the first time that we said it to one another would be a momentous occasion, the kind of story that when told would make our sons roll their eyes and pretend to throw up and our daughters say, "Wow, that's so romantic." Hoping to make it that kind of an occasion, I planned to say it on our six-month anniversary at the restaurant where we had our first date.

Of course, you had other ideas. Two nights before, you had said it to me while we were watching the news, casually, as if it were the most natural thing in the world. I was so surprised that all I could do was kiss you and say, "I'm so happy."

Maybe it was revenge or maybe you misheard me, but when I finally said it between the appetizers and main course, all you said was, "Wow, the food is as wonderful as I remembered it. Wasn't it good? Doesn't it make you happy?"

Mutter (verb)

After being together for years, we stopped fighting with one another. Fighting was for people who still cared for one another, who still had passion buried beneath layers of familiarity and routine. Fighting always ended with making up with one another, one of the few things that television and movie writers got right.

Instead, we merely argued. We argued about little things, big things, and everything in-between. Because there was very little passion and emotion underlying our arguments, the right side, the logical side always won out. But that didn't stop either of us from saying a few choice words under our breath as we each went off to do something more productive, more satisfying.

There was never really a winner in any of our arguments, only more reasons to resent one another.

Neck (noun; verb)

I loved your whole body, but I loved that most of all. While most people loved the more obvious parts, which I myself enjoyed as well, there was something about that small part of you that connected your head to your shoulders that drove me wild. I liked kissing it and running my fingers along it. When you got cold or when you were ticklish, small goose bumps would appear all over your body, but nowhere would they be more pronounced than in that area from your ears down to the top of your shoulders. Sometimes, when you were fast asleep, I would blow on it gently, watching the small hairs vibrate ever so slightly in the dim light of our bedroom.

Ostracize (verb)

For whatever reason, most of our mutual friends—not the ones we had each brought with us into the relationship, but the ones that we had accumulated together over time—chose you. It did not make any sense to me, because you were the one who had been unfaithful. You were the one who had turned your back on us in the most cowardly of ways. And yet, they did not have any problem inviting you and forgetting about me when it came to dinner parties, picnics, and holiday events. The only time I managed to see any of them was when it was my turn to take Maria to a playdate (though this rarely happened given that you nixed most of these playdates, saying that Maria could not attend because she was spending the weekend with her father).

"I haven't seen you in so long. You have to come around more often. I'll give you a call."

"Of course," I would say, knowing that it would never happen.

Pisces (noun)

My mother, who thought that all forms of religion consisted of nothing more than brainwashing and spiritual conditioning, believed zealously that astrology was the only way to determine romantic compatibility. She was convinced that the stars were sentient beings that arranged themselves in particular patterns so as to communicate with us. They stayed in particular formations for millennia, or until we figured out exactly what it was that they were trying to communicate. I learned early on in my childhood that questioning this belief would only lead to a harsh scolding.

When you told my mother your sign, she shook her head and said, "That simply won't work. My son is an Aries. It will only end in heartbreak."

"Nonsense," you said. "What utter nonsense." You called my mother a quack and a nut. She just sat there and smiled, waiting for you to run out of steam. Her unresponsiveness only fueled your anger more.

On the subway ride home, you kept at it, wondering what planet my mother was from. "How could someone believe in that nonsense?" you asked. "I am so glad that you didn't end up a freak like her."

I just waited for you to run out of steam.

Quill (noun)

The first time that I came back to your apartment, I noticed that your bookshelf was full of Shakespeare. You had different versions of his completed works—the Oxford, Yale, and Pelican—as well as numerous books about his life and work. Although I never felt any real emotional connection to his work, I could see that you did, so I memorized a sonnet for our next date. At first, you did not understand what I was saying, unable to process the words coming out of my mouth. It was understandable—like many who had spent most of their high school English classes either asleep or smoking behind the school, I was under the mistaken impression that each of the line breaks required a pause of some sort.

But once I managed to fumble through the first few lines, it was clear that you understood what I was saying. By the time I finished, you were beaming and you jumped into my arms and kissed me.

At that moment, I wanted to thank "him" for expressing things in a way that I could never hope to.

Retarded (noun; adjective)

The moment the word escaped my lips, I knew it was a mistake. Your sister had Down syndrome, and while you were okay with the occasional use of the word to describe a stupid situation, you vehemently hated its use as an insult.

Your face contorted in rage and disgust, as if I had called you a bitch or a whore.

"How could you say that? Get out!" you screamed. You looked as if you would have thrown something at me if something were near.

I wanted to say sorry, but I was not sure that I actually was. So I grabbed my coat and left, wondering why I had not just gone ahead and called you a bitch and a whore as well.

Singed (verb)

You laughed as you poured me some red wine, showing me burns on your index finger and along your forearm. It was the first time that you had ever cooked a full meal and you had been careless with the oven and the stove. As you sipped your wine, you recounted your struggles with the chicken and the asparagus, and the way that you had to check constantly to see if the pie was burnt.

"And my hair!"

I thought it was so cute the way that you held up your long brown hair. I thought it was still beautiful, but you jumped out of your seat and said you had to cut it right away or else. I did not know what the "or else" meant, or why you needed to cut off your hair right away given that your hair was burned, not on fire. I wanted more than anything to ask for some of the strands so that I could commemorate the meal in some way. It seemed like an appropriate thing to do, given that you could not preserve pieces of dry chicken or asparagus between pages of an old hardcover.

I really wish I had. That way, I would have had some proof other than our beautiful daughter that our marriage had moments of happiness.

Tuesday (noun)

Cheap movie night was the perfect date night for us. Our therapist said that we needed to try to do things that would rekindle our feelings for one another. For $500/hour, she recommended that we revisit the places where we fell in love and start taking up activities that we could learn together. She assured us that, in her professional opinion, doing these sorts of things would go a long way to helping us mend our relationship and ultimately save our marriage. But after some awkward dinners at chic restaurants full of people who still loved each other, and some drunken nights with our friends playing trivia and charades, we decided that movies would be the best way to rekindle our missing spark. What better way to learn to appreciate one another than by sitting in a dark room for hours, never having to talk to one another other than to ask for popcorn or candy?

Ulcer (noun)

When I came home from the hospital and explained what had happened, you wrapped your arms around me and said not to worry. You would find a job so that I could find a less stressful one, maybe work at a non-profit or government agency. There were plenty of places that I could work that would not be as taxing as a corporate law firm (and maybe I could actually do some good with my law degree as I had originally intended when I first decided that I wanted to be an attorney).

"We can manage. All we have to do is be more careful with our expenses."

When I told Maria that I was quitting my job to find something else, she did not understand.

"But Daddy, if you quit your job, how will we live?"

"I'm going to find another job and your Mom is going to find a job as well."

"But what kind of job can Mommy get? She doesn't know how to do anything."

Voldemort (noun)

You loved the books as much as I did, but you could not stand the movies. You said that you were tired of Hollywood butchering yet another fantasy world and you refused to take Maria to see any of them. I want her to appreciate books more than stupid movies, you said. I'm not going to raise an idiot for a daughter.

I completely disagreed, argued that she loved the books, the movies, the whole Harry Potter world. She wasn't going to stop reading because she watched the movies. The movies would only make her want to read and reread the books even more.

"No," you said. "End of discussion."

When you found out later that I had taken her to see the movies behind your back, you took my copies of *The Lord of the Rings* and replaced them with DVDs.

"This will save us space in the long run," you said. "We might as well start now."

Wrapping (noun; adjective; verb)

I was never good at wrapping gifts, so the first few that I gave you I simply put in gift bags and covered with tissue paper. One day, in passing, you mentioned how much you loved the act of tearing open gifts, especially because you had rarely been able to as a child. Your parents had often struggled with keeping jobs, so many birthdays and Christmases passed with you having nothing to open. It meant that whenever you did receive a present, the act of opening it up was as important as the gift itself.

So the next gift I got you, a microwave because yours had stopped working, I wrapped in newspaper. I still could not wrap my head around spending money on something that would end up in the trash (an argument that I would later use as to why I never bought you flowers). Unfortunately, the newspaper tore multiple times and I had to eventually cover the box with three layers of newspaper.

When you saw it, you told me how sweet I was. You loved crossword puzzles and thanked me for wrapping a gift in such a thoughtful manner. You carefully removed the crossword portion and tore off the rest.

I had no problem taking credit for the lucky break.

Xylophone (noun)

Maria was definitely your daughter, as she was as musically *un*gifted as you. She could only hum two notes, struggled with a recorder, and could not clap or tap a steady beat. When she sang along with the other children at school musicals, parents in the audience cringed. Those parents who knew us looked over with such pity. She has no business being in a music school, their looks said. Who cared that none of their children would grow up to be Edith Piaf or Yo-Yo Ma? All they saw was a girl who made noise instead of music.

When her teacher asked us if we could help Maria choose an instrument so that she could still participate in school functions, we thought that we would let her decide. Although she enjoyed pulling strings and blowing into different instruments, she enjoyed banging away with the fuzzy mallets most of all. Our late nights were never the same again.

Yellow (noun; adjective; verb)

I had a collection of bright fluorescent hoodies that I used to wear in college. I had stopped wearing them long ago but left them boxed up in my closet because I could not bear to part with them. What I did not know was that you had donated all of them without telling me and had left the box sitting in the closet in the hopes that I would never find out. When I finally did, after discovering the empty box when I needed a hoodie with my college's name plastered along the front for my 10th year reunion, I was furious. "How could you?" I asked. "I loved those hoodies."

"Whoops," you said, shrugging your shoulders. "I promise not to do it again."

Zipper (noun)

There was no emotion involved. I was feeling lonely after you had moved out, taking so many of the things we had filled our home with you, including Maria. I spent many nights wondering if I had made a mistake. So many marriages were able to survive adultery. Why not us?

One night, after a firm cocktail hour, I could not bear to go home alone. Long after everyone from work had left, I started talking to someone sitting at the bar. So after I bought her a few drinks, I invited her to come back with me. When she stepped inside, she knew exactly what was going on, seeing the half-filled rooms with pictures and cardboard boxes scattered throughout.

When it was finished, she smiled, put her clothing back on, and kissed my cheek.

"Good luck," she said. "It'll be okay."

All I could do was nod and show her the way out.

About the Author

Cedrick Mendoza-Tolentino was a 2014 Emerging Writer's Fellow at the Center for Fiction in New York City. He graduated with honors in the Undergraduate Creative Writing Program at Columbia University. He has had work published in *Liars' League New York, Akashic - Mondays are Murder, Gargoyle Magazine, Joyland, Slow Trains* and *Plain Spoke*. His chapbook *Alphabetica: The Other Side of Love* was published by Corgi Snorkel Press.

About the Press

Unsolicited Press based out of Portland, Oregon and focuses on the works of the unsung and underrepresented. As a womxn-owned, all-volunteer small publisher that doesn't worry about profits as much as championing exceptional literature, we have the privilege of partnering with authors skirting the fringes of the lit world. We've worked with emerging and award-winning authors such as Shann Ray, Amy Shimshon-Santo, Brook Bhagat, Kris Amos, and John W. Bateman.

Learn more at unsolicitedpress.com. Find us on twitter and instagram.